The Fate of a Crown

The Fate of a Crown

a Crown

L. Frank Baum

MINT EDITIONS

The Fate of a Crown was first published in 1905.

This edition published by Mint Editions 2021.

ISBN 9781513211787 | E-ISBN 9781513210582

Published by Mint Editions®

 MINT
EDITIONS

minteditionbooks.com

Publishing Director: Jennifer Newens
Design & Production: Rachel Lopez Metzger
Project Manager: Micaela Clark
Typesetting: Westchester Publishing Services

A List of Chapters

I

The Blue Envelope

Leaning back in my chair, I smoked my morning cigar and watched Uncle Nelson open his mail. He had an old-fashioned way of doing this: holding the envelope in his left hand, clipping its right edge with his desk shears, and then removing the inclosure and carefully reading it before he returned it to its original envelope. Across one end he would make a memorandum of the contents, after which the letters were placed in a neat pile.

As I watched him methodically working, Uncle Nelson raised a large blue envelope, clipped its end, and read the inclosure with an appearance of unusual interest. Then, instead of adding it to the letters before him, he laid it aside; and a few minutes later reverted to it again, giving the letter a second careful perusal. Deeply musing, for a time he sat motionless in his chair. Then, arousing himself from his deep abstraction, he cast a fleeting glance in my direction and composedly resumed his task.

I knew Uncle Nelson's habits so well that this affair of the blue envelope told me plainly the communication was of unusual importance. Yet the old gentleman calmly continued his work until every letter the mail contained was laid in a pile before him and fully docketed. With the last he suddenly swung around in his chair and faced me.

"Robert," said he, "how would you like to go to Brazil?"

Lacking a ready answer to this blunt question I simply stared at him.

"De Pintra has written me," he continued—"do you know of Dom Miguel de Pintra?" I shook my head. "He is one of the oldest customers of the house. His patronage assisted us in getting established. We are under deep obligations to de Pintra."

"I do not remember seeing his name upon the books," I said, thoughtfully.

"No; before you came into the firm he had retired from business—for he is a wealthy man. But I believe this retirement has been bad for him. His energetic nature would not allow him to remain idle, and he has of late substituted politics for business."

"That is not so bad," I remarked, lightly. "Some people make a business of politics, and often it proves a fairly successful one."

My uncle nodded.

"Here in New Orleans, yes," he acknowledged; "but things are vastly different in Brazil. I am sorry to say that Dom Miguel is a leader of the revolutionists."

"Ah," said I, impressed by his grave tone. And I added: "I have supposed that Dom Pedro is secure upon his throne, and personally beloved by his subjects."

"He is doubtless secure enough," returned Uncle Nelson, dryly, "but, although much respected by his people, there is, I believe, serious opposition to an imperial form of government. Rebellions have been numerous during his reign. Indeed, these people of Brazil seem rapidly becoming republicans in principle, and it is to establish a republican form of government that my friend de Pintra has placed himself at the head of a conspiracy."

"Good for de Pintra!" I cried, heartily.

"No, no; it is bad," he rejoined, with a frown. "There is always danger in opposing established monarchies, and in this case the Emperor of Brazil has the countenance of both Europe and America."

As I ventured no reply to this he paused, and again regarded me earnestly.

"I believe you are the very person, Robert, I should send de Pintra. He wishes me to secure for him a secretary whom he may trust implicitly. At present, he writes me, he is surrounded by the emperor's spies. Even the members of his own household may be induced to betray him. Indeed, I imagine my old friend in a very hot-bed of intrigue and danger. Yet he believes he could trust an American who has no partiality for monarchies and no inducement to sympathize with any party but his own. Will you go, Robert?"

The question, abrupt though it was, did not startle me. Those accustomed to meet Nelson Harcliffe's moods must think quickly. Still, I hesitated.

"Can you spare me, Uncle?"

"Not very well," he admitted. "You have relieved me of many of the tedious details of business since you came home from college. But, for de Pintra's sake, I am not only willing you should go, but I ask you, as a personal favor, to hasten to Rio and serve my friend faithfully, protecting him, so far as you may be able, from the dangers he is facing. You will find him a charming fellow—a noble man, indeed—and he needs just such a loyal assistant as I believe you will prove. Will you go, Robert?"

Uncle Nelson's sudden proposal gave me a thrill of eager interest best explained by that fascinating word "danger." Five minutes before I would have smiled at the suggestion that I visit a foreign country on so quixotic an errand; but the situation was, after all, as simple as it was sudden in development, and my uncle's earnest voice and eyes emphasized his request in no uncertain manner. Would I go? Would I, a young man on the threshold of life, with pulses readily responding to the suggestion of excitement and adventure, leave my humdrum existence in a mercantile establishment to mingle in the intrigues of a nation striving to cast off the shackles of a monarchy and become free and independent? My answer was assured.

Nevertheless, we Harcliffes are chary of exhibiting emotion. Any eagerness on my part would, I felt, have seriously displeased my reserved and deliberate uncle. Therefore I occupied several minutes in staring thoughtfully through the open window before I finally swung around in my chair and answered:

"Yes, Uncle, I will go."

"Thank you," said he, a flush of pleasure spreading over his fine old face. Then he turned again to the letter in the blue envelope. "The Castina sails on Wednesday, I see, and Dom Miguel wishes his new secretary to go on her. Therefore you must interview Captain Lertine at once, and arrange for passage."

"Very well, sir."

I took my hat, returned my uncle's grave bow, and left the office.

II

Valcour

The Castina was a Brazilian trading-ship frequently employed by the firm of Harcliffe Brothers to transport merchandise from New Orleans to Rio de Janiero. I had formed a slight acquaintance with the master, Pedro Lertine, and was not surprised when he placed his own state-room at my disposal; for although the vessel usually carried passengers, the cabin accommodations were none of the best.

The Captain asked no questions concerning my voyage, contenting himself with the simple statement that he had often carried my father with him in the Castina in former years, and was now pleased to welcome the son aboard. He exhibited rare deference toward my uncle, Nelson Harcliffe, as the head of our firm, when the old gentleman came to the head of the levee to bid me good by; this Uncle Nelson did by means of a gentle pressure of my hand. I am told the Harcliffes are always remarkable for their reserve, and certainly the head of our house was an adept at repressing his emotions. Neither he nor my father, who had been his associate in founding the successful mercantile establishment, had ever cared to make any intimate friends; and for this reason the warmth of friendship evinced by Uncle Nelson in sending me on this peculiar mission to Dom Miguel de Pintra had caused me no little astonishment.

After his simple handshake my uncle walked back to his office, and I immediately boarded the Castina to look after the placing of my trunks. Before I had fairly settled myself in my cozy state-room we were under way and steaming down the river toward the open sea.

On deck I met a young gentleman of rather prepossessing personality who seemed quite willing to enter into conversation. He was a dark-eyed, handsome Brazilian, well dressed and of pleasing manners. His card bore the inscription, *Manuel Cortes de Guarde*. He expressed great delight at finding me able to speak his native tongue, and rendered himself so agreeable that we had soon established very cordial relations. He loved to talk, and I love to listen, especially when I am able to gather information by so doing, and de Guarde seemed to know Brazil perfectly, and to delight in describing it. I noticed that he never touched on politics, but from his general conversation I gleaned considerable knowledge of the country I was about to visit.

During dinner he chattered away continually in his soft Portuguese patois, and the other passengers, less than a dozen in number, seemed content to allow him to monopolize the conversation. I noticed that Captain Lertine treated de Guarde with fully as much consideration as he did me, while the other passengers he seemed to regard with haughty indifference. However, I made the acquaintance of several of my fellow-voyagers and found them both agreeable and intelligent.

I had promised myself a pleasant, quiet voyage to the shores of Brazil, but presently events began to happen with a rapidity that startled me. Indeed, it was not long before I received a plain intimation that I had embarked upon an adventure that might prove dangerous.

We were two days out, and the night fell close and warm. Finding my berth insufferably oppressive I arose about midnight, partially dressed, and went on deck to get whatever breeze might be stirring. It was certainly cooler than below, and reclining in the shadow beside a poop I had nearly succeeded in falling asleep when aroused by the voices of two men who approached and paused to lean over the taffrail. They proved to be Captain Lertine and de Guarde, and I was about to announce my presence when the mention of my own name caused me to hesitate.

"I cannot understand why you should suspect young Harcliffe," the Captain said.

"Because, of all your passengers, he would be most fitted to act as de Pintra's secretary," was the reply. "And, moreover, he is a Harcliffe."

"That's just it, senhor," declared the other; "he is a Harcliffe, and since his father's death, one of the great firm of Harcliffe Brothers. It is absurd to think one of his position would go to Brazil to serve Miguel de Pintra."

"Perhaps the adventure entices him," returned de Guarde's soft voice, in reflective tones. "He is but lately from college, and his uncle may wish him to know something of Brazil, where the greater part of the Harcliffe fortune has been made."

"*Deus Meo!*" exclaimed the Captain; "but you seem to know everything about everybody, my dear Valcour! However, this suspicion of young Harcliffe is nonsense, I assure you. You must look elsewhere for the new secretary—provided, of course, he is on my ship."

"Oh, he is doubtless on board," answered de Guarde, with a low, confident laugh. "De Pintra's letters asked that a man be sent on the first ship bound for Rio, and Nelson Harcliffe is known to act promptly in all business matters. Moreover, I have studied carefully the personality of each of your passengers, and none of them seems fitted for the post so perfectly as young Harcliffe himself. I assure you, my dear Lertine, that I am right. He can be going out for no other purpose than to assist de Pintra."

The Captain whistled softly.

"Therefore?" he murmured.

"Therefore," continued de Guarde, gravely, "it is my duty to prevent his reaching his destination."

"You will have him arrested when we reach Rio?"

"Arrested? No, indeed. Those Americans at Washington become peevish if we arrest one of their citizens, however criminal he may be. The situation demands delicate treatment, and my orders are positive. Our new secretary for the revolution must not reach Rio."

Again the Captain whistled—a vague melody with many false and uncertain notes. And the other remained silent.

Naturally I found the conversation most interesting, and no feeling of delicacy prevented my straining my ears to catch more of it. It was the Captain who broke the long silence.

"Nevertheless, my dear Valcour—"

"De Guarde, if you please."

"Nevertheless, de Guarde, our Mr. Harcliffe may be innocent, and merely journeying to Brazil on business."

"I propose to satisfy myself on that point. Great God, man! do you think I love this kind of work—even for the Emperor's protection? But my master is just, though forced at times to act with seeming cruelty. I must be sure that Harcliffe is going to Brazil as secretary to the rebel leader, and you must aid me in determining the fact. When our man goes to breakfast in the morning I will examine his room for papers. The pass-key is on the bunch you gave me, I suppose?"

"Yes, it is there."

"Very well. Join your passengers at breakfast, and should Mr. Harcliffe leave the table on any pretext, see that I am duly warned."

"Certainly, senhor."

"And now I am going to bed. Goodnight, Lertine."

"Goodnight, de Guarde."

They moved cautiously away, and a few minutes later I followed, regaining my state-room without encountering anyone.

Once in my bunk I lay revolving the situation in my mind. Evidently it was far from safe to involve one's self in Brazilian politics. My friend Valcour, as the Captain had called him, was a spy of the Emperor, masquerading under the title of Senhor Manuel Cortes de Guarde. A clever fellow, indeed, despite his soft, feminine ways and innocent chatter, and one who regarded even murder as permissible in the execution of his duty to Dom Pedro. It was the first time in my life I had been, to my knowledge, in any personal danger, and the sensation was rather agreeable than otherwise.

It astonished me to discover that de Guarde knew so perfectly the contents of Dom Miguel's letter to my uncle. Doubtless the secret police had read and made a copy of it before the blue envelope had been permitted to leave Brazil. But in that case, I could not understand why they had allowed the missive to reach its destination.

In his cool analysis of the situation, my friend the spy had unerringly hit upon the right person as the prospective secretary of the revolutionary leader. Yet he had no positive proof, and it was pleasant to reflect that in my possession were no papers of any sort that might implicate me. Uncle Nelson had even omitted the customary letter of introduction.

"De Pintra knew your father, and your face will therefore vouch for your identity," the old gentleman had declared. Others have remarked upon the strong resemblance I bear my father, and I had no doubt de Pintra would recognize me. But, in addition, I had stored in my memory a secret word that would serve as talisman in case of need.

The chances of my puzzling Dom Pedro's detective were distinctly in my favor, and I was about to rest content in that knowledge, when an idea took possession of me that promised so much amusement that I could not resist undertaking it. It may be that I was influenced by a mild chagrin at the deception practised upon me by de Guarde, or the repulsion that a secret-service man always inspires in the breast of a civilian. Anyway, I resolved to pit my wits against those of Senhor Valcour, and having formulated my plan I fell asleep and rested comfortably until daybreak.

It had been my habit to carry with me a pocket diary, inscribing therein any vivid impressions or important events that occurred to me. There were many blank pages, for my life had been rather barren of incident of late; but I had resolved to keep a record of this trip and for this purpose the little book was now lying upon the low shelf that served as table in my room.

Arising somewhat before my usual hour I made a hurried toilet and sat down to make entries in my diary. I stated that my sudden desire to visit Brazil was due to curiosity, and that my uncle had placed several minor business matters in my hands to attend to. My return to New Orleans would depend entirely upon how well I liked the country where our house had so successfully traded for a half-century. Arriving at this point, I added the following paragraphs:

"On the ship with me Uncle Nelson is sending a private secretary to Dom Miguel de Pintra, who, it seems, was an ancient customer of our house, but is now more interested in politics than in commerce. This secretary is a remarkable fellow, yet so placid and unassuming that no one is likely to suspect his mission. He seems to know everything, and has astonished me by his intimate knowledge of all that transpires upon the ship. For example, he tells me that my friend de Guarde, of whom I have already grown fond, is none other than a certain Valcour, well known in the secret service of his majesty the Emperor of Brazil. Valcour is on board because he knows the contents of a letter written by de Pintra to my uncle, asking for a shrewd American to become his private secretary; also Valcour is instructed to dispose of the rebel secretary before we land at Rio—meaning, of course, to murder him secretly. This seemingly horrible plot but amuses our secretary, for Valcour has only poor Captain Lertine to aid him, whereas the wonderful American has a following of desperate men trained to deeds of bloodshed who will obey his slightest nod. From what I learn I am confident the plan is to assassinate my friend Valcour in a secret manner, for here is a rare opportunity to rid themselves of a hated royalist spy. Poor de Guarde! I would like to warn him of his danger, but dare not. Even then, I doubt his ability to escape. The toils are closing about him, even while he innocently imagines that he, as the Emperor's agent, controls the situation. It would all be laughable, were it not so very terrible in its tragic aspect.

"But there! I must not mix with politics, but strive to hold aloof from either side. The secretary, though doubtless a marvel of diplomacy and duplicity, is too unscrupulous to suit me. He has actually corrupted the entire crew, from the engineers down, and at his word I am assured the fellows would mutiny and seize the ship. What chance has my poor friend de Guarde—or Valcour—to escape this demon? Yet, after all, it is not my affair, and I dare not speak."

This entry I intended to puzzle Senhor Valcour, even if it failed to wholly deceive him. I wrote it with assumed carelessness, to render it uniform with the former paragraphs the book contained. These last were of a trivial nature, dating back for some months. They would interest no one but myself; yet I expected them to be read, for I left the diary lying upon my shelf, having first made a number of pin-marks in the paint, at the edges of the cover, so that I might assure myself, on my return to the room, whether or not the book had been disturbed.

This task completed, I locked the door behind me and cheerfully joined the breakfast party in the main cabin.

De Guarde was not present, but no one seemed to miss him, and we lingered long in light conversation over the meal, as it is the custom of passengers aboard a slow-going ship.

Afterward, when I went on deck, I discovered de Guarde leaning over the rail, evidently in deep thought. As I strolled past him, puffing my cigar, he turned around, and the sight of his face, white and stern, positively startled me. The soft dark eyes had lost their confident, merry look, and bore a trace of fear. No need to examine the pin-marks on my shelf. The Emperor's spy had, without doubt, read the false entry in my diary, and it had impressed him beyond my expectation.

III

A Good Republican

During the remainder of the voyage I had little intercourse with Senhor Manuel Cortes de Guarde. Indeed, I had turned the tables quite cleverly upon the spy, who doubtless imagined many dangers in addition to those indicated in my diary. For my part, I became a bit ashamed of the imposition I had practised, despite the fact that the handsome young Brazilian had exhibited a perfect willingness to assassinate me in the Emperor's interests. Attracted toward him in spite of my discoveries, I made several attempts to resume our former friendly intercourse; but he recoiled from my overtures and shunned my society.

In order to impress upon de Guarde the truth of the assertions I had made in the diary I selected a young physician, a Dr. Neel, to impersonate the intriguing and bloodthirsty American secretary. He was a quiet, unobtrusive fellow, with an intelligent face, and a keen, inquiring look in his eyes. I took occasion to confide to Dr. Neel, in a mysterious manner that must have amused him, that I was afflicted with an incomprehensible disease. He promptly mistook me for a hypochondriac, and humored me in a good-natured fashion, so that we were frequently observed by de Guarde in earnest and confidential conversation. My ruse proved effective. Often I surprised a look of anxiety upon the Brazilian's face as he watched Dr. Neel from a distance; but de Guarde took pains not to mingle with any group that the physician made part of, and it was evident the detective had no longer any desire to precipitate a conflict during the voyage to Rio.

I do not say that Valcour was cowardly. In his position I am positive I could not have escaped the doubts that so evidently oppressed him. He secluded himself in his state-room, under pretense of illness, as we drew nearer to Brazil, and I was considerably relieved to have him out of the way.

Captain Lertine, to whom Valcour had evidently confided his discovery of the diary, was also uneasy during those days, and took occasion to ask me many questions about Dr. Neel, which I parried in a way that tended to convince him that the physician was none other than the secret emissary sent by my uncle to Miguel de Pintra. The good Captain was nervous over the safety of the ship, telling me in a confidential way that nearly all his crew were new hands, and that he had no confidence in their loyalty to the Emperor.

His face bore an expression of great relief when we anchored in the bay of Rio de Janiero on a clear June morning at daybreak, and no time was lost in transferring the passengers of the Castina to a small steam launch, which soon landed us and our effects upon the quay.

I had not seen Valcour since we anchored, but after bidding good by to Dr. Neel, who drove directly to his hotel, I caught a glimpse of the detective's eager face as he followed the doctor in a cab.

The whole affair struck me as being a huge joke, and the sensation of danger that I experienced on board the ship was dissolved by the bright sunshine and the sight of the great city calmly awakening and preparing for its usual daily round of business.

I dispatched my trunks to the Continental Railway station, and finding that I had ample time determined to follow them on foot, the long walk being decidedly grateful after the days on shipboard. Much as I longed to see the beauties of Brazil's famous capital, I dared not at this time delay to do so, as my uncle had impressed upon me the necessity of presenting myself to de Pintra as soon as possible after my arrival.

Another thing that influenced me was the deception that I had practised upon the detective. Valcour, with the Emperor at his back, was now a power to be reckoned with, and as soon as he discovered that I had misled him the police would doubtless be hot upon my trail. So my safest plan was to proceed at once to the province where my new chief had power to protect me.

I reached the railway station without difficulty and found I had a quarter of an hour to spare.

"Give me a ticket to Cuyaba," I said to the clerk at the window.

He stared at me as he handed the card through the grating.

"Matto Grosso train, senhor," he said. "It leaves at eight o'clock."

"Thank you," I returned, moving away.

A tall policeman in an odd uniform of black and gold barred my way.

"Your pardon, senhor Americano," said he, touching his visor in salute; "I beg you to follow me quietly."

He turned on his heel and marched away, and I, realizing that trouble had already overtaken me, followed him to the street.

A patrol was drawn up at the curb, a quaint-looking vehicle set low between four high wheels and covered with canvas. Startled at the sight I half turned, with a vague idea of escape, and confronted two stout policemen at my rear.

Resistance seemed useless. I entered the wagon, my captor seating himself upon the bench beside me. Instantly we whirled away at a rapid pace.

I now discerned two men, also in uniform, upon the front seat. One was driving the horses, and presently the other climbed over the seat and sat opposite my guard.

The tall policeman frowned.

"Why are you here, Marco?" he demanded, in a threatening voice.

"For this!" was the prompt answer; and with the words I caught a quick flash as the man called Marco buried a knife to the hilt in the other's breast.

My captor scarce uttered a sound as he pitched headforemost upon the floor of the now flying wagon. The driver had but given a glance over his shoulder and lashed his horses to their utmost speed.

Cold with horror at the revolting deed I gazed into the dark eyes of the murderer. He smiled as he answered my look and shrugged his shoulders as if excusing the crime.

"A blow for freedom, senhor!" he announced, in his soft, native patois. "Dom Miguel would be grieved were you captured by the police."

I started.

"Dom Miguel! You know him, then?"

"Assuredly, senhor. You are the new secretary. Otherwise you would not be so foolish as to demand a ticket to Cuyaba—the seat of the revolution."

"I begin to understand," I said, after a moment's thought. "You are of the police?"

"Sergeant Marco, senhor; at your service. And I have ventured to kill our dear lieutenant in order to insure your safety. I am sorry," he added, gently touching the motionless form that lay between us; "the lieutenant was a good comrade—but a persistent royalist."

"Where are you taking me?" I asked.

"To a suburban crossing, where you may catch the Matto Grosso train."

"And you?"

"I? I am in no danger, senhor. It is you who have done this cruel deed—and you will escape. The driver—a true patriot—will join me in accusing you."

I nodded, my horror of the tragedy growing each moment. Truly this revolutionary party must be formed of desperate and unscrupulous men, who hesitated at no crime to advance their interests. If the royalists were but half so cruel I had indeed ventured into a nest of adders. And it was the thought of Valcour's confessed purpose to murder me on shipboard that now sealed my lips from a protest against this deed that was to be laid upon my shoulders.

Presently the wagon slowed up, stopping with a jerk that nearly threw me from my seat. The sergeant alighted and assisted me to follow him.

We were at a deserted crossing, and the buildings of the city lay scattered a quarter of a mile away.

"Take this flag, senhor. The engineer will stop to let you aboard. Farewell, and kindly convey my dutiful respects to Dom Miguel."

As the wagon rolled away the train came gliding from the town, and I stepped between the tracks and waved the flag as directed. The engine slowed down, stopped a brief instant, and I scrambled aboard as the train recovered speed and moved swiftly away.

For the present, at least, I was safe.

Quite unobtrusively I seated myself in the rear end of the passenger coach and gazed from the window as we rushed along, vainly endeavoring to still the nervous beating of my heart and to collect and center my thoughts upon the trying situation in which I found myself. Until the last hour I had been charmed with my mission to Brazil, imagining much pleasure in acting as secretary to a great political leader engaged in a struggle for the freedom of his country. The suggestion of danger my post involved had not frightened me, nor did it even now; but I shrank from the knowledge that cold-blooded assassination was apparently of little moment to these conspirators. In less than two hours after landing at Rio I found myself fleeing from the police, with a foul and revolting murder fastened upon me in the name of the revolution! Where would it all end? Did Uncle Nelson thoroughly realize the terrible nature of the political plot into which he had so calmly thrust me? Probably not. But already I knew that Brazil was a dangerous country and sheltered a hot-headed and violent people.

It was a long and dreary ride as we mounted the grade leading to the tablelands of the interior. Yet the country was beautifully green and peaceful under the steady glare of the sun, and gradually my distress passed away and left me more composed.

Neither the passengers nor trainmen paid the slightest attention to me, and although at first I looked for arrest at every station where we halted, there was no indication that the police of Rio had discovered my escape and flight.

Night came at last, and I dozed fitfully during the long hours, although still too nervous for sound sleep. We breakfasted at a way-station, and a couple of hours later, as I was gazing thoughtfully out the window, the conductor aroused me by settling into the seat at my side. He was a short, pudgy individual, and wheezed asthmatically with every breath.

"I received a telegram at the last station," he confided to me, choking and coughing between the words. "It instructed me to arrest an American senhor traveling to Cuyaba. Have you seen him?"

I shivered, and stared back into his dull eyes.

"Ah! I thought not," he continued, with a short laugh. "It is not the first telegram they have sent this trip from Rio, you know; but I cannot find the fellow anywhere aboard. Do you wonder? How can I be expected to distinguish an American from a Brazilian? Bah! I am not of the police."

I began to breathe again. The conductor nudged my ribs with his elbow.

"These police will perhaps be at the station. Cuyaba is the next stop. But we will slow up, presently, at a curve near the edge of the forest. Were I the American, and aboard this train, I would get out there, and wait among the trees in the forest until Dom Miguel's red cart comes along. But, *ai de mim*, the American is not here! Eh? Thank God for it! But I must leave, senhor. Good day to you."

He bustled away, and at once I seized my traveling-bag and slipped out to the back platform. We slowed up at the curve a moment later, and I sprang to the ground and entered the shade of a group of trees that marked the edge of the little forest.

And there I sat upon a fallen tree-trunk for two weary hours, wondering what would happen next, and wishing with all my heart I had never ventured into this intrigue-ridden country. But at the end of that time I heard the rattle of a wagon and the regular beat of a horse's feet.

Peering from my refuge I discerned a red cart slowly approaching over the road that wound between the railway track and the forest. It was driven by a sleepy Brazilian boy in a loose white blouse and a wide straw hat.

As he arrived opposite me I stepped out and hailed him.

"Are you from Dom Miguel de Pintra?" I asked.

He nodded.

"I am the American he is expecting," I continued, and climbed to the seat beside him. He showed no surprise at my action, nor, indeed, any great interest in the meeting; but as soon as I was seated he whipped up the horse, which developed unexpected speed, and we were soon rolling swiftly over the country road.

IV

The Chieftain

The province of Matto Grosso is very beautiful, the residences reminding one greatly of English country estates, except that their architecture is on the stiff Portuguese order. At least a half-mile separated the scattered mansions from one another, and the grounds were artistically planned and seemingly well cared for. At this season the rich, luxuriant foliage of Brazil was at its best, and above all brooded a charming air of peace that was extremely comforting after my late exciting experiences. We met few people on the way, and these were peasants, who touched their hats respectfully as we passed.

We had driven some five miles when we came to an estate rather more extensive than its neighbors, for the hedge of blooming cactus that divided the grounds from the roadway ran in an unbroken line as far as the eye could reach.

However, we came to a gateway at last and turned into the grounds, where magnificent trees shaded a winding drive ascending to the fine old mansion of de Pintra.

A man stood upon the porch shading his eyes with his hand and gazing at us as we approached. When I alighted from the cart he came down the steps to meet me, bowing very courteously, and giving my hand a friendly pressure. No other person was in sight, and the red cart had disappeared around the corner of the house.

"You are welcome, sir," he said, in a quiet but most agreeable voice. "You come from my friend Nelson Harcliffe? That was my thought." He paused to give me a keen look, and then smiled—a sweet, winning smile such as I have seldom seen. "Ah! may you not be a Harcliffe yourself? Your features seem quite familiar. But, pardon me, sir; I have not introduced myself. I am Miguel de Pintra."

I fear I stared at him with somewhat rude intentness, for Dom Miguel was a man to arouse interest in any beholder. Tall, spare, but not ungraceful, his snow-white hair and beard made strong contrast with his bronzed features. His eyes, soft and gentle in expression, were black. His smile, which was not frequent, disclosed a line of even, white teeth. His dress was a suit of plain, well-fitting black, supplemented by irreproachable linen. Taken altogether, Dom Miguel appeared a model of the old school of gentility, which may be as quickly recognized in Brazil as in England, France or America. Indeed, it seemed an absurdity to connect this eminently respectable personage with revolutions, murders, and intrigue, and my spirits rose the moment I set eyes upon his pleasant face.

"I am Robert Harcliffe," said I, answering the question his politeness would not permit him to ask; "the son of Marshall Harcliffe."

A flash of surprise and delight swept over his dark face. He seized both my hands in his own.

"What!" he cried, "Nelson Harcliffe has sent me his own nephew, the son of my dear old friend? This is, indeed, a rare expression of loyalty!"

"I thought you knew," I rejoined, rather embarrassed, for the fathomless eyes were reading me with singular eagerness.

"I only knew that Nelson Harcliffe would respond promptly to my requests. I knew that the Castina would bring my secretary to Brazil. But whom he might be I could not even guess." He paused a moment, to continue in a graver tone: "I am greatly pleased. I need a friend—a faithful assistant."

"I hope I may prove to be both, sir," I returned, earnestly. "But you seem not to lack loyal friends. On my way hither from Rio de Janiero I have been protected more than once, doubtless by your orders."

"Yes; the cause has many true adherents, and I notified our people to expect an American gentleman on the Castina and to forward him to me in safety. They know, therefore, that you came to assist the Revolution, and it would have been strange, indeed, had the royalists been able to interfere with you."

"Your party is more powerful than I had suspected," I remarked, thinking of my several narrow escapes from arrest.

"We are only powerful because the enemy is weak," answered Dom Miguel, with a sigh. "Neither side is ready for combat, or even an open rupture. It is now the time of intrigue, of plot and counterplot, of petty conspiracies and deceits. These would discourage any honest heart were not the great Cause behind it all—were not the struggle for freedom and our native land! But come; you are weary. Let me show you to your room, Robert Harcliffe."

He dwelt upon the name with seeming tenderness, and I began to understand why my father and my stern Uncle Nelson had both learned to love this kindly natured gentleman of Brazil.

He led me through cool and spacious passages to a cozy room on the ground floor, which, he told me, connected by a door with his study or work-room.

"I fear my trunks have been seized by the government," said I, and then related to him the details of my arrest and the assassination of the police lieutenant.

He listened to the story calmly and without interruption; but when it was finished he said:

"All will be reported to me this evening, and then we will see whether your baggage cannot be saved. There were no papers that might incriminate you?"

"None whatever."

Then I gave him the story of Valcour, or de Guarde, and he smiled when I related the manner in which the fellow had been deceived.

"I knew that Valcour had been dispatched to intercept my secretary," said he, "and you must know that this personage is not an ordinary spy, but attached to the Emperor himself as a special detective. Hereafter," he continued, reflectively, "the man will be your bitter enemy; and although you have outwitted him once he is a foe not to be despised. Indeed, Harcliffe, your post is not one of much security. If, when I have taken you fully into our confidence, you decide to link your fortunes to those of the Revolution, it will be with the full knowledge that your life may be the forfeit. But there—we will speak no more of business until after dinner."

He left me, then, with many cordial expressions of friendship.

A servant brought my luncheon on a tray, and after eating it I started for a stroll through the grounds, enjoying the fragrance and brilliance of the flowers, the beauties of the shrubbery, and the stately rows of ancient trees. The quiet of the place suggested nothing of wars and revolutions, and it was with real astonishment that I reflected that this establishment was the central point of that conspiracy whose far-reaching power had been so vividly impressed upon me.

Engaged in this thought I turned the corner of a hedge and came face to face with a young girl, who recoiled in surprise and met my gaze with a sweet embarrassment that caused me to drop my own eyes in confusion.

"Your pardon, senhorita!" I exclaimed, and stood aside for her to pass.

She nodded, still searching my face with her clear eyes, but making no movement to proceed. I noted the waves of color sweeping over her fair face and the nervous tension of the little hands that pressed a mass of flowers to her bosom. Evidently she was struggling for courage to address me; so I smiled at her, reassuringly, and again bowed in my best manner, for I was not ill pleased at the encounter.

I have always had a profound reverence for woman—especially those favored ones to whom Nature has vouchsafed beauty in addition to the charm of womanhood. And here before me stood the most beautiful girl I had ever seen, a type of loveliness more sweet and delightful than any I had even dreamed could exist.

It was my fate to recognize this in the moments that I stood watching her lips tremble in the endeavor to form her first words to me.

"You are the American?" she asked, finally.

"Assuredly, donzella. Permit me to introduce myself. I am Robert Harcliffe."

"My uncle expected you," she said, shyly.

"Your uncle?"

"Dom Miguel is not really my uncle," answered the girl; "but he permits me to call him so, since he is my guardian. Yet it was not from him I learned of your arrival, but from Francisco, who traveled from Rio on the same train."

My face doubtless showed that I was puzzled, for she added, quickly:

"Francisco is my brother, senhor. We are both devoted heart and soul to the Cause. That is why I felt that I must speak with you, why I must welcome you to our fellowship, why I must implore you to be strong and steadfast in our behalf!"

I smiled at the vehemence that had vanquished her former hesitation, and to my delight her exquisite face lighted with an answering smile.

"Ah, you may laugh at me with impunity, senhor Americano, for I have intuitions, and they tell me you will be faithful to the cause of freedom. Nay, do not protest. It is enough that I have read your face."

With this she made a pretty courtesy and vanished around the hedge before I could summon a word to detain her.

It is astonishing to what an extent this encounter aroused my enthusiasm for "the Cause." Heretofore I had regarded it rather impersonally, as an affair in which I had engaged at the request of my good uncle. But now that I had met this fellow-conspirator and gazed into the enchanting depths of her eyes, I was tremendously eager to prove my devotion to the cause of freedom.

True, I had seen the girl but a few moments. Even her name was unknown to me. But she was a rebel; Francisco, her brother, was a rebel;

and Dom Miguel permitted her to call him "uncle." Very good; very good, indeed!

When I returned to my room I was surprised to find my trunks there, they having arrived in some mysterious way during my brief absence.

I dressed for dinner and found my way to the drawing-room, where my host—or my employer, rather—was conversing with a lady and a gentleman.

There was no reason my heart should give that bound to warn me; no one could fail to recognize that slender, graceful figure, although it was now enveloped in dainty folds of soft white mulle. But she had no intention of allowing her chance meeting to stand for a formal introduction, and as Dom Miguel presented me she shot a demure yet merry glance at me from beneath her long lashes that might readily have effected my conquest had I not already surrendered without discretion.

"The Senhorita Lesba Paola," announced de Pintra, speaking the name with evident tenderness. Then he turned to the man. "Senhor Francisco Paola," said he.

Francisco Paola puzzled me at that first meeting nearly as much as he did later. His thin form was dressed in a dandified manner that was almost ludicrous, and the fellow's affectation was something amazing. Somewhat older than his bewitching sister, his features were not without a sort of effeminate beauty, of which he seemed fully aware. At once I conceived him to be a mere popinjay, and had no doubt he would prove brainless and well-nigh insufferable. But Dom Miguel introduced Paola with grave courtesy and showed him so much deference that I could not well be ungracious to the young dandy. Moreover, he had a stronger claim to my toleration: he was Lesba's brother.

Scarcely were these introductions complete when another lady entered the room. She gave a slight start at sight of me, and then advanced gracefully to Dom Miguel's side.

"My daughter, Mr. Harcliffe; Senhora Izabel de Mar," said he, and gave me a curious glance that I could not understand.

I looked at Madam Izabel and lowered my eyes before the cold and penetrating stare I encountered. She was handsome enough, this woman; but her features, however regular, were repellant because of their absolute lack of expression—a lack caused by repression more than a want of mobility. Her face seemed carved of old ivory. Even the great eyes were impenetrable, reflecting nothing of the emotions that might dwell within. I found myself shivering, and although I sincerely tried to be agreeable to Dom Miguel's daughter, the result was little more than farcical.

My sudden appearance in the household had evidently caused Madam Izabel surprise; perhaps it annoyed her, as well. But she drew me to a seat beside her and plied me with questions which I was at a loss how to answer, in view of the supposedly private nature of my mission to Brazil. Inwardly I blamed Dom Miguel for not telling me how far his daughter and his guests were in his confidence; but before I blundered more than a few aimless sentences a light voice interrupted us and Francisco Paola leaned over Madam Izabel's chair with a vapid compliment on the lady's charms and personal appearance that was fairly impertinent in its flippancy.

The look she gave him would have silenced an ordinary man; but Senhor Francisco smiled at her frown, took the fan from her hand, and wielded it in a mincing manner, pouring into her unwilling ears a flood of nonsense that effectually cut me out of the conversation.

Dom Miguel came to my relief by requesting me to take the younger lady in to dinner, and to my surprise Madam Izabel took Paola's arm without apparent reluctance and followed us to the dining-room.

The repast would have been, I fear, rather stupid, but for Senhor Francisco's ceaseless chatter. To my great disappointment the donzella Lesba Paola appeared exceedingly shy, and I could scarce recognize in her my eager questioner of the afternoon. De Pintra, indeed, courteously endeavored to draw the ladies into a general conversation; but his daughter was cold and unresponsive, and the host himself appeared to be in a thoughtful mood. For my part, I was glad to have the fop monopolize the conversation, while I devoted my attention to the silent girl beside me; but it was evident that a general feeling of relief prevailed when the ladies returned to the drawing-room and left us to our cigars and wine.

When the servants had been dismissed and we three men were alone, Dom Miguel addressed me with unrestrained frankness.

"I suppose you know little of our revolutionary movement, Mr. Harcliffe," he began.

"Very little, indeed," I responded, briefly.

"It dates back for several years, but has only recently attained to real importance. Gradually our people, of all degrees, have awakened to the knowledge that they must resist the tyranny of the imperial government, with its horde of selfish and unscrupulous retainers. The Emperor is honest enough, but weak, and his advisors leave him no exercise of his own royal will. Spurred by the nation's distress, the Revolution has at last taken definite form, and at present centers in me. But as our strength grows our danger increases. The existing government, knowing itself threatened, has become keen to ferret out our secrets and to discover the leaders of the Cause, that they may crush all with one blow." He paused, and flicked the ash from his cigar with a thoughtful gesture. "For this, and many another reason, I need the assistance of a secretary whom I may trust implicitly—who will, if need be, die rather than betray my confidence."

I glanced hesitatingly at the man opposite me. It seemed strange that Dom Miguel should speak of these personal matters before a third party.

Paola was trying to balance a spoon upon the edge of his glass. He met my gaze with the usual vacant smile upon his face, yet in the instant I caught a gleam in his eye so shrewd and comprehensive that it positively startled me. Instantly his face was shrouded in a cloud of smoke from his cigar, and when it cleared away the idiotic leer that appeared upon his countenance indicated anything rather than intelligence.

Dom Miguel looked from one to the other of us and smiled.

"Perhaps I should tell you," said he, earnestly, "that no man is higher in our counsels or more thoroughly esteemed by all classes of patriots than Francisco Paola. You may speak in his presence with entire freedom."

At this the popinjay twisted the end of his moustache and bowed with mock dignity. I stared at him with an astonishment tinged with disgust. His eyes were now glassy and his gaze vacuous. The eternal smile expressed merely stupidity and conceit.

I turned to Dom Miguel, who gravely awaited my reply.

"Sir," said I, "you are my father's old friend. My uncle, who was my father's partner and is now my own associate in business, sent me to you with the injunction to serve you to the best of my ability. This, by way of gratitude for many favors shown our house by you in the days when a friend counted largely for success. Being an American, I love freedom. Your cause shall be my cause while I remain with you. Of my power to serve you there may be question; but my loyalty you need never doubt."

Dom Miguel reached across the table and grasped my hand warmly. Paola poured himself a glass of wine and drank to me with a nod of his head.

"When first I saw you," said de Pintra, with emotion, "I knew we had gained a strong ally, and God knows we need trustworthy friends at this juncture. The great Revolution, which is destined some day to sweep Brazil from Para to Rio Grande do Sul, is now in my keeping. In my possession are papers wherein are inscribed the names of the patriots who have joined our Cause; to me has been intrusted the treasure accumulated for years to enable us to carry out our plans. Even those plans—carefully formulated and known to but a few of my associates, the trusted leaders—are confided to my care. I cannot risk a betrayal that would imperil the Revolution itself and destroy all those concerned in it, by employing for secretary a Brazilian, who might become a spy of Dom Pedro, or be frightened by threats and imprisonment."

Leaning forward, he regarded me earnestly. His eyes, so gentle in repose, now searched my own with fierce intensity.

"I cannot even trust my own household," he whispered; "my own flesh and blood has been suspected of treason to the Cause. There are spies everywhere, of both sexes, among the lowly and the gentle. So I accept your services, Robert Harcliffe, and thank you in the name of the Revolution."

It was all rather theatric, but I could not question the sincerity of his speech, and it succeeding in impressing me with the gravity of my new position.

"Come," said Paola, breaking the tense pause, "let us rejoin the ladies."

Five minutes later he was at the piano, carolling a comic ditty, and I again wondered what element this seemingly brazen and hollow vessel might contain that could win the respect of a man like Miguel de Pintra. Evidently I must, to some extent, glean a definite knowledge of the Revolution and its advocates through a process of absorption. This would require time, as well as personal contact with Dom Miguel and his confrères, and my only hope of mastering the situation lay in a careful study of each personage I met and a cautious resistance of any temptation to judge them hastily. Nevertheless, this mocking, irrepressive Francisco Paola had from the first moment of his acquaintance become an astounding puzzle to me, and so far I could see no indication of any depths to his character that could explain the esteem in which he was held by the chief.

But now his sister's sweet, upturned face drew me to her side, and I straightway forgot to dwell upon the problem.

V

Madam Izabel

I slept well in my pleasant room, but wakened early, the bright sunshine pouring in at my open window and the songs of many birds sounding a lively chorus.

After a simple toilet I sprang through a low window to the ground and wandered away among the flowers and shrubbery. It was in my thoughts to revisit the scene of my first meeting with Lesba, but I had no hope of finding her abroad at that hour until I caught a glimpse of her white gown through a small arbor. The vision enchanted me, and after pausing a moment to feast my eyes upon her loveliness, I hastily approached to find her cutting roses for the breakfast-table. She greeted me in her shy manner, but in a way that made me feel I was not intruding. After a few conventional remarks she asked, abruptly:

"How do you like Dom Miguel?"

"Very much," said I, smiling at her eagerness. "He seems eminently worthy of the confidence reposed in him by his compatriots."

"He is a born leader of men," she rejoined, brightly, "and not a rebel of us all would hesitate to die for him. How do you like my brother?"

I was sorry she asked the question, for its abruptness nearly took my breath away, and I did not wish to grieve her. To gain time I laughed, and was answered with a frown that served to warn me.

"Really, donzella," I made haste to say, "if I must be quite frank, your brother puzzles me. But I think I shall like him when I understand him better."

She shook her head as if disappointed.

"No one ever understands Francisco but me," she returned, regretfully.

"Does he understand himself?" I foolishly asked.

The girl looked at me with a gleam of contempt.

"Sir, my brother's services are recognized throughout all Brazil. Even Fonseca respects his talents, and the suspicious Piexoto trusts him implicitly. Francisco's intimate friends positively adore him! Ah, senhor, it is not necessary for his sister to sing his praises."

I bowed gravely.

"Let me hope, donzella, that your brother will soon count me among his intimates." It was the least I could say in answer to the pleading look in her eyes, and to my surprise it seemed to satisfy her, for she blushed with pleasure.

"I am sure he likes you already," she announced; "for he told me so as he bade me good by this morning."

"Your brother has gone away?"

"He started upon his return to court an hour ago."

"To court!" I exclaimed, amazed at his audacity.

She seemed amused.

"Did you not know, senhor? Francisco Paola is Dom Pedro's Minister of Police."

I acknowledged that the news surprised me. That the Emperor's Minister of Police should be a trusted leader of the Revolutionary party seemed incomprehensible; but I had already begun to realize that extraordinary conditions prevailed in Brazil. Perhaps the thing that caused me most astonishment was that this apparently conceited and empty-headed fellow had ever been selected for a post so important as Minister of Police. Yet the fact explained clearly how I had received secret protection from the moment of my landing at Rio until I had joined Dom Miguel.

The girl was laughing at me now, and her loveliness made me resolve not to waste more of these precious moments in political discussion. She was nothing loath to drop the subject, and soon we were chattering merrily of the flowers and birds, the dewdrops and the sunshine, and all those inconsequent things that are wont to occupy youthful lips while hearts beat fast and glances shyly mingle. When, at length, we sauntered up the path to breakfast I had forgotten the great conspiracy altogether, and congratulated myself cordially upon the fact that Lesba and I were well on the way to becoming good friends.

Madam Izabel did not appear at the morning meal, and immediately it was over Dom Miguel carried me to his study, where he began to acquaint me thoroughly with the standing and progress of the proposed revolution, informing me, meantime, of my duties as secretary.

While we were thus occupied the door softly opened and Izabel de Mar entered.

She cast an odd glance in my direction, bowed coldly to her father, and then seated herself at a small table littered with papers.

A cloud appeared upon Dom Miguel's brow. He hesitated an instant, and then addressed her in a formal tone.

"I shall not need you today, Izabel."

She turned upon him with a fierce gesture.

"The letters to Piexoto are not finished, sir," she exclaimed.

"I know, Izabel; I know. But Mr. Harcliffe will act as my secretary, hereafter; therefore he will attend to these details."

She rose to her feet, her eyes flashing, but her face as immobile as ever.

"I am discharged?" she demanded.

"Not that, Izabel," he hastened to reply. "Your services have been of inestimable value to the Cause. But they are wearing out your strength, and some of our friends thought you were too closely confined and needed rest. Moreover, a man, they considered—"

"Enough!" said she, proudly. "To me it is a pleasure to toil in the cause of freedom. But my services, it seems, are not agreeable to your leaders—rather, let us say, to that sly and treacherous spy, Francisco Paola!"

His face grew red, and I imagined he was about to reply angrily; but the woman silenced him with a wave of her hand.

"O, I know your confidence in the Emperor's Minister, my father; a confidence that will lead you all to the hangman, unless you beware! But why should I speak? I am not trusted, it seems; I, the daughter of de Pintra, who is chief of the Revolution. This foreigner, whose heart is cold in our Cause, is to take my place. Very well. I will return to the court—to my husband."

"Izabel!"

"Do not fear. I will not betray you. If betrayal comes, look to your buffoon, the Minister of Police; look to your cold American!"

She pointed at me with so scornful a gesture that involuntarily I recoiled, for the attack was unexpected. Then my lady stalked from the room like a veritable queen of tragedy.

Dom Miguel drew a sigh of relief as the door closed, and rubbed his forehead vigorously with his handkerchief.

"That ordeal is at last over," he muttered; "and I have dreaded it like a coward. Listen, senhor! My daughter, whose patriotism is not well understood, has been suspected by some of my associates. She has a history, has Izabel—a sad history, my friend." For a moment Dom Miguel bowed his face in his hands, and when he raised his head again the look of pained emotion upon his features lent his swarthy skin a grayish tinge.

"Years ago she loved a handsome young fellow, one Leon de Mar—of French descent, who is even now a favorite with the Emperor," he resumed. "Against my wishes she married him, and her life at the court proved a most unhappy one. De Mar is a profligate, a rake, a gamester, and a scoundrel. He made my daughter suffer all the agonies of hell. But she uttered no complaint and I knew nothing of her sorrow. At last, unable to bear longer the scorn and abuse of her husband, Izabel came to me and confessed the truth, asking me to give her the shelter of a home. That was years ago, senhor. I made her my secretary, and found her eager to engage in our patriotic conspiracy. It is my belief that she has neither seen nor heard from de Mar since; but others have suspected her. It is hard indeed, Robert, not to be suspicious in this whirlpool of intrigue wherein we are engulfed. A few weeks ago Paola swore that he found Izabel in our garden at midnight engaged in secret conversation with that very husband from whom she had fled. I have no doubt he was deceived; but he reported it to the Secret Council, which instructed me to confide no further secrets to my daughter, and to secure a new secretary as soon as possible. Hence my application to your uncle, and your timely arrival to assist me."

He paused, while I sat thoughtfully considering his words.

"I beg that you will not wrong my daughter with hasty suspicions," he continued, pleadingly. "I do not wish you to confide our secrets to her, since I have myself refrained from doing so, out of respect for the wishes of my associates. But do not misjudge Izabel, my friend. When the time comes for action she will be found a true and valuable adherent to the Cause. And now, let us to work!"

I found it by no means difficult to become interested in the details of the plot to overthrow the Emperor Dom Pedro and establish a Brazilian Republic. It was amazing how many great names were enrolled in the Cause and how thoroughly the spirit of freedom had corrupted the royal army, the court, and even the Emperor's trusted police. And I learned, with all this, to develop both admiration and respect for the man whose calm judgment had so far directed the mighty movement and systematized every branch of the gigantic conspiracy. Truly, as my fair Lesba had said, Dom Miguel de Pintra was "a born leader of men."

Night after night there assembled at his house groups of conspirators who arrived secretly and departed without even the servants having knowledge of their visit. During the counsels every approach to the house was thoroughly guarded to ward against surprise.

Strong men were these republican leaders; alert, bold, vigilant in serving the Cause wherein they risked their lives and fortunes. One by one I came to know and admire them, and they spoke freely in my presence and trusted me. Through my intercourse with these champions of liberty, my horizon began to broaden, thus better fitting me for my duties.

Francisco Paola, the Emperor's Minister, came frequently to the conferences of the Secret Council. Always he seemed as simpering, frivolous, and absurd as on the day I first met him. To his silly jokes and inconsequent chatter none paid the slightest attention; but when a real problem arose and they turned questioningly to Paola, he would answer in a few lightly spoken words that proved at once shrewd and convincing. The others were wont to accept his decisions with gravity and act upon them.

I have said that Paola impressed me as being conceited. This might well be true in regard to his personal appearance, his social accomplishments—playing the piano and guitar, singing, riding, and the like—but I never heard him speak lightly of the Cause or boast of his connection with it. Indeed, he exhibited a queer mingling of folly and astuteness. His friends appeared to consider his flippancy and self-adulation as a mask that effectually concealed his real talents. Doubtless the Emperor had the same idea when he made the fellow his Minister of Police. But I, studying the man with fervid interest, found it difficult to decide whether the folly was a mask, or whether Paola had two natures—the second a sub-conscious intelligence upon which he was able to draw in a crisis.

He certainly took no pains to impress anyone favorably, and his closest friends were, I discovered, frequently disgusted by his actions.

From the first my judgment of the man had been influenced by his sister's enthusiastic championship. Lesba seemed fully in her brother's confidence, and although she was not a recognized member of the conspiracy, I found that she was thoroughly conversant with every detail of our progress. This information must certainly have come from Francisco, and as I relied absolutely upon Lesba's truth and loyalty, her belief in her brother impressed me to the extent of discrediting Madam Izabel's charge that he was a traitor.

Nevertheless, Paola had acted villainously in thrusting this same charge upon a woman. What object, I wondered, could he have in accusing Izabel to her own father, in falsely swearing that he had seen her in conversation with Leon de Mar—the man from whose ill treatment she had fled?

Madam Izabel had not returned to the court, as she had threatened in her indignant anger. Perhaps she realized what it would mean to place herself again within the power of the husband she had learned to hate and despise. She still remained an inmate of her father's mansion, cold and impassive as ever. Dom Miguel treated her with rare consideration on every occasion of their meeting, seeking to reassure her as to his perfect faith in her loyalty and his sorrow that his associates had cast a slur upon her character.

To me the chief was invariably kind, and his gentleness and stalwart manhood soon won my esteem. I found myself working for the good of the cause with as much ardor as the most eager patriot of them all, but my reward was enjoyed as much in Lesba's smiles as in the approbation of Dom Miguel.

That the government was well aware of our plot there was no question. Through secret channels we learned that even the midnight meetings of the Secret Council were known to the Emperor. The identity of the leaders had so far been preserved, since they came masked and cloaked to the rendezvous, but so many of the details of the conspiracy had in some way leaked out that I marveled the Emperor's heavy hand had not descended upon us long ago. Of course de Pintra was a marked man, but they dared not arrest him until they had procured all the information they desired, otherwise they would defeat their own purpose.

One stormy night, as I sat alone with Dom Miguel in his study, I mentioned my surprise that in view of the government's information of our plot we were not summarily arrested. It was not a council night, and we had been engaged in writing letters.

"I suppose they fear to precipitate trouble between such powerful factions," he answered, somewhat wearily. "The head of the conspiracy is indeed here, but its branches penetrate to every province of the country, and were an outbreak to occur here the republicans of Brazil would rise as one man. Dom Pedro, poor soul, does not know where to look for loyal support. His ministry is estranged, and he is not even sure of his army."

"But should they discover who our leaders are, and capture them, there would be no one to lead the uprising," I suggested.

"True," assented the chief. "But it is to guard against such a coup that our Council is divided into three sections. Only one-third of the leaders could be captured at anyone time. But I do not fear such an attempt, as every movement at the capital is reported to me at once."

"Suppose they were to strike you down, sir. What then? Who would carry out your plans? Where would be the guiding hand?"

For a moment he sat thoughtfully regarding me.

"I hope I shall be spared until I have accomplished my task," he said, at length. "I know my danger is great; yet it is not for myself I fear. Lest the Cause be lost through premature exposure, I have taken care to guard against that, should the emergency arise. Light me that candle yonder, Robert, and I will reveal to you one of our most important secrets."

He motioned toward the mantel, smiling meantime at my expression of surprise.

I lighted the candle, as directed, and turned toward him expectantly. He drew a rug from before the fireplace, and stooping over, touched a button that released a spring in the flooring.

A square aperture appeared, through which a man might descend, and peering over his shoulder I saw a flight of stairs reaching far downward.

De Pintra turned and took the candle from my hand.

"Follow me," he said.

VI

The Secret Vault

The stairs led us beneath the foundations of the house and terminated in a domed chamber constructed of stone and about ten feet in diameter.

In the floor of this chamber was a trapdoor, composed of many thicknesses of steel, and so heavy that it could be raised only by a stout iron windlass, the chain of which was welded to a ring in the door's face.

Dom Miguel handed me the candle and began turning the windlass. Gradually but without noise the heavy door of metal rose, and disclosed a still more massive surface underneath.

This second plate, of highly burnished steel, was covered with many small indentations, of irregular formation. It was about three feet square and the curious indentations, each one of which had evidently been formed with great care, were scattered over every inch of the surface.

"Put out the light," said de Pintra.

I obeyed, leaving us in total darkness.

Next moment, as I listened intently, I heard a slight grating noise, followed by a soft shooting of many bolts. Then a match flickered, and Dom Miguel held it to the wick and relighted the candle.

The second door had swung upward upon hinges, showing three iron steps that led into a vault below.

The chief descended and I followed; not, however, without a shuddering glance at the great door that stood suspended as if ready to crash down upon our heads and entomb us.

Just within the entrance an electric light, doubtless fed by a storage battery, was turned on, plainly illuminating the place.

I found the vault lined with thick plates of steel, riveted firmly together. In the center was a small table and two wooden stools. Shelves were ranged around the walls and upon them were books, papers, and vast sums of money, both in bank-notes and gold.

"Here," said my companion, glancing proudly around him, "are our sinews of war; our records and funds and plans of operation. Should Dom Pedro's agents gain access to this room they would hold in their hands the lives and fortunes of many of the noblest families in Brazil—

and our conspiracy would be nipped in the bud. You may know how greatly I trust you when I say that even my daughter does not guess the existence of this vault. Only a few of the Secret Council have ever gained admittance here, and the secret of opening the inner door is known only to myself and one other—Francisco Paola."

"Paola!" I exclaimed.

"Yes; it was he who conceived the idea of this vault; it was his genius that planned a door which defies any living man to open without a clear knowledge of its secret. Even he, its inventor, could not pass the door without my assistance; for although he understands the method, the means are in my possession. For this reason I alone am responsible for the safe-keeping of our records and treasure."

"The air is close and musty," said I, feeling oppressed in breathing.

He looked upward.

"A small pipe leads to the upper air, permitting foul vapors to escape," said he; "but only through the open door is fresh air admitted. Perhaps there should be better ventilation, yet that is an unimportant matter, for I seldom remain long in this place. It is a store-house—a secret crypt—not a work-room. My custom has been to carry all our records and papers here each morning, after they have been in use, that they may be safe from seizure or prying eyes. But such trips are arduous, and I am not very strong. Therefore I will ask you to accompany me, hereafter."

"That I shall do willingly," I replied.

When we had passed through the door on our return the chief again extinguished the light while he manipulated the trap. Afterward the windlass allowed the outer plate of metal to settle firmly into place, and we proceeded along the passage and returned to the study.

Many trips did I make to the secret vault thereafter, but never could I understand in what manner the great door of shining steel was secured, as Dom Miguel always opened and closed it while we were in total darkness.

As the weeks rolled by I not only became deeply interested in my work, but conceived a still greater admiration for the one man whose powerful intelligence directed what I knew to be a gigantic conspiracy.

Spies were everywhere about Dom Miguel. One day we discovered his steward—an old and trusted retainer of the family—to be in the Emperor's pay. But de Pintra merely shrugged his shoulders and said nothing. Such a person could do little to imperil the cause, for its important secrets could not be surprised. The grim vault guarded them well.

My duties occupying me only at night, my days were wholly my own, and they passed very pleasantly indeed, for my acquaintance with Lesba Paola had ripened into a close friendship between us—a friendship I was eager to resolve into a closer relation.

But Lesba, although frank and ingenuous in all our intercourse, had an effectual way of preventing the declarations of love which were ever on my tongue, and I found it extremely difficult to lead our conversation into channels that would give me an opportunity to open my heart to her.

She was an expert horsewoman, and we took many long rides together, during which she pointed out to me the estates of all the grandees in the neighborhood. Dom Miguel, whose love for the beautiful girl was very evident, seemed to encourage our companionship, and often spoke of her with great tenderness.

He would dwell with especial pride upon the aristocratic breeding of his ward, which, to do him justice, he valued more for its effect upon other noble families than for any especial advantage it lent to Lesba herself; for while Dom Miguel was thoroughly republican in every sense of the word, he realized the advantages to be gained by interesting the best families of Brazil in the fortunes of his beloved Cause, and one by one he was cleverly succeeding in winning them. My familiarity with the records taught me that the Revolution was being backed by the flower of Brazilian nobility—the most positive assurance in my eyes of the justice and timeliness of the great movement for liberty. The idea that monarchs derive their authority from divine sources—so prevalent amongst the higher classes—had dissolved before the leader's powerful arguments and the object lessons Dom Pedro's corrupt ministry constantly afforded. All thoughtful people had come to a realization that liberty was but a step from darkness into light, a bursting of the shackles that had oppressed them since the day that Portugal had declared the province of Brazil an Empire, and set a scion of her royal family to rule its people with autocratic sway.

And Lesba, sprung from the bluest blood in all the land, had great influence in awakening, in those families she visited, an earnest desire for a republic. Her passionate appeals were constantly inspiring her fellows with an enthusiastic devotion to the cause of liberty, and this talent was duly appreciated by Dom Miguel, whose admiration for the girl's simple but direct methods of making converts was unbounded.

"Lesba is a rebel to her very finger-tips," said he, "and her longing to see her country a republic is exceeded by that of no man among us.

But we are chary of admitting women to our councils, so my little girl must be content to watch for the great day when the cause of freedom shall prevail."

However, she constantly surprised me by her intimate knowledge of our progress. As we were riding one day she asked:

"Were you not impressed by your visit to the secret vault?"

"The secret vault!" I exclaimed. "Do you know of it?"

"I can explain every inch of its construction," she returned, with a laugh; "everything, indeed, save the secret by means of which one may gain admission. Was it not Francisco's idea? And is it not exceedingly clever?"

"It certainly is," I admitted.

"It was built by foreign workmen, brought to Brazil secretly, and for that very purpose. Afterward the artisans were sent home again; and not one of them, I believe, could again find his way to my uncle's house, for every precaution was taken to prevent their discovering its location."

"That was well done," said I.

"All that Francisco undertakes is well done," she answered simply.

This faith in her perplexing brother was so perfect that I never ventured to oppose it. We could not have remained friends had I questioned either his truth or ability.

Madam Izabel I saw but seldom, as she avoided the society of the family and preferred the seclusion of her own apartments. On the rare occasions of our meeting she treated me with frigid courtesy, resenting any attempt upon my part to draw her into conversation.

For a time it grieved me that Dom Miguel's daughter should regard me with so much obvious dislike and suspicion. Her sad story had impressed me greatly, and I could understand how her proud nature had resented the slanders of Francisco Paola, and writhed under them. But one evening an incident occurred that served to content me with Madame Izabel's aversion, and led me to suspect that the Minister of Police had not been so guilty as I had deemed him.

It was late, and Dom Miguel had preceded me to the domed chamber while I carried the records and papers to be deposited within the vault.

After raising the first trap my employer, as usual, extinguished the candle. I heard the customary low, grating noise, but before the shooting of the bolts reached my ears there was a sharp report, followed by a vivid flash, and turning instantly I beheld Madam Isabel standing beside us, holding in her hand a lighted match and peering eagerly at the surface of the trap.

My eyes followed hers, and while Dom Miguel stood as if petrified with amazement I saw the glitter of a gold ring protruding from one of the many curious indentations upon the plate. The next instant the match was dashed from her grasp and she gave a low cry of pain.

"Light the candle!" commanded de Pintra's voice, fiercely.

I obeyed. He was holding the woman fast by her wrist. The ring had disappeared, and the mystery of the trap seemed as inscrutable as ever.

Dom Miguel, greatly excited and muttering imprecations all the way, dragged his daughter through the passage and up the stairs. I followed them silently to the chief's study. Then, casting the woman from him, de Pintra confronted her with blazing eyes, and demanded:

"How dare you spy upon me?"

Madam Izabel had become cool as her father grew excited. She actually smiled—a hard, bitter smile—as she defiantly looked into his face and answered:

"Spy! You forget, sir, that I am your daughter. I came to your room to seek you. You were not here; but the door to this stairway was displaced, and a cold air came through it. Fearing that some danger menaced you I passed down the stairs until, hearing a noise, I paused to strike a match. You can best explain the contretemps."

Long and silently Dom Miguel gazed upon his daughter. Then he said, abruptly, "Leave the room!"

She bowed coldly, with a mocking expression in her dark eyes, and withdrew.

As she passed me I noted upon her cheeks an unwonted flush that rendered her strikingly beautiful.

Deep in thought de Pintra paced the floor with nervous strides. Finally he turned toward me.

"What did you see?" he asked, sharply.

"A ring," I answered. "It lay upon the trap, and the stone was fitted into one of the numerous indentations."

He passed his hand over his brow with a gesture of despair.

"Then she saw it also," he murmured, "and my secret is a secret no longer."

I remained silent, looking upon him curiously, but in deep sympathy.

Suddenly he held out his hand. Upon the little finger was an emerald ring, the stone appearing to be of no exceptional value. Indeed, the trinket was calculated to attract so little attention that I had barely noticed it before, although I remembered that my employer always wore it.

"This," said he, abruptly, "is the key to the vault."

I nodded. The truth had flashed upon me the moment Madam Izabel had struck the match. And now, looking at it closely, I saw that the stone was oddly cut, although the fact was not likely to impress one who was ignorant of the purpose for which it was made.

The chief resumed his pacing, but presently paused to say:

"If anything happens to me, my friend, be sure to secure this ring above all else. Get it to Paola, or to Fonseca, or Piexoto as soon as possible—you know where they may be found. Should it fall into the hands of the royalists the result would be fatal."

"But would either of your associates be able to use the ring, even if it passed into their possession?" I asked.

"There are two hundred indentations in the door of the trap," answered de Pintra, "and the stone of the ring is so cut that it fits but one of these. Still, if our friends have time to test each cavity, they are sure to find the right one, and then the stone of my ring acts as a key. My real safety, as you will observe, lay in the hope that no one would discover that my ring unlocked the vault. Now that Izabel has learned the truth I must guard the ring as I would my life—more, the lives of all our patriotic band."

"Since you suspect her loyalty, why do you not send your daughter away?" I suggested.

"I prefer to keep her under my own eye. And, strange as her actions of tonight seem, I still hesitate to believe that my own child would conspire to ruin me."

"The secret is not your own, sir," I ventured to say.

"True," he acknowledged, flushing deeply, "the secret is not my own. It belongs to the Cause. And its discovery would jeopardize the revolution itself. For this reason I shall keep Izabel with me, where, admitting she has the inclination to betray us, she will not have the power."

After this night he did not extinguish the light when we entered the vault, evidently having decided to trust me fully; but he took pains to secure the trap in the study floor so that no one could follow us. After watching him apply the key several times I became confident that I could find the right indentation without trouble should the occasion ever arise for me to unlock the vault unaided.

Days passed by, and Madam Izabel remained as quiet and reserved as if she had indeed abandoned any further curiosity concerning the secret vault. As for my fellow-rebel, the Senhorita Lesba, I rode and chatted with her in the firm conviction that here, at least, was one secret connected with the revolution of which she was ignorant.

VII

General Fonseca

One evening, as I entered Dom Miguel's library, I found myself face to face with a strange visitor. He did not wear a mask, as did so many of the conspirators, even in the chief's presence; but a long black cloak swept in many folds from his neck to his feet.

My first thought was to marvel at his size, for he was considerably above six feet in height and finely proportioned, so that his presence fairly dominated us and made the furnishings of the room in which he stood seem small and insignificant.

As I entered, he stood with his back to the fireplace confronting Dom Miguel, whose face wore a sad and tired expression. I immediately turned to withdraw, but a gesture from the stranger arrested me.

"Robert," said Dom Miguel, "I present you to General Manuel Deodoro da Fonseca."

I bowed profoundly. General Fonseca was not only a commander of the Emperor's royal army, but Chief Marshal of the forces of the Revolutionary party. I had never seen the great man before, as his duties required his constant presence at the capital; but no figure loomed larger than his in the affairs of the conspiracy.

Seldom have I met with a keener or more disconcerting glance than that which shot from his full black eyes as I stood before him. It seemed to search out my every thought, and I had the sensation of being before a judge who would show no mercy to one who strove to dissemble in his presence.

But the glance was brief, withal. In a moment he had seized my hand and gripped it painfully. Then he turned to Dom Miguel.

"Let me hear the rest of your story," said he.

"There is nothing more, General. Izabel has learned my secret, it is true; but she is my daughter. I will vouch for her faith."

"Then will not I!" returned Fonseca, in his deep, vibrant tones. "Never have I believed the tale of her estrangement from that scoundrel, Leon de Mar. Men are seldom traitors, for they dare not face the consequences. Women have no fear of man or devil. They are daughters of Delilah—each and everyone."

He turned suddenly to me.

"Will you also vouch for Senhora Izabel de Mar?" he asked.

"No," I answered.

"And quite right, sir," he returned, with a grim smile. "Never trust a woman in politics. But how about Francisco Paola? Do you vouch for him?"

I hesitated, startled by the question.

"Answer me!" he commanded.

"I cannot see that I am required to vouch for anyone, General," said I, nettled by his manner. "I am here to serve the Cause, not to judge the loyalty of its leaders."

"Ugh!" said he, contemptuously; and I turned my back upon him, facing Dom Miguel, over whose features a fleeting smile passed.

Fonseca stalked up and down the apartment, his sword clanking beneath his cloak, and his spurs clicking like castanets. Then he planted his huge figure before the chief.

"Watch them both," said he brusquely; "your daughter and your friend. They are aware of our most important secrets."

De Pintra's face reddened.

"Francisco is true as steel," he retorted, firmly. "Not one of us—including yourself, General—has done more to serve the Cause. I have learned to depend upon his discretion as I would upon my own—or yours."

The general frowned and drew a folded paper from his breast pocket.

"Read that," said he, tossing it into Dom Miguel's hand. "It is a copy of the report made by Paola to the Emperor this morning."

De Pintra glanced at the paper and then gave it to me, at the same time dropping his head in his hands.

I read the report. It stated that the Minister of Police had discovered the existence of a secret vault constructed beneath the mansion of Miguel de Pintra, the rebel chief. This vault, the police thought, contained important records of the conspiracy. It was built of double plates of steel, and the entrance was guarded by a cleverly constructed door, which could only be unlocked by means of a stone set in a ring which was constantly worn by Dom Miguel himself. In conclusion the minister stated that every effort was being made to secure possession of the ring, when the rebels would be at the Emperor's mercy.

"Well, sir, what do you think of Francisco Paola now?" inquired Fonseca, with a significant smile.

"Did he not himself invent the secret vault?" I asked.

"He did, sir."

"How long ago."

"A matter of two years. Is it not so, Dom Miguel?"

The chief bowed.

"And until now Paola has kept this secret?" I continued.

"Until now, yes!" said the general. "Until the vault was stored with all our funds and the complete records of the revolution."

"Then it seems clear to me that Paola, as Minister of Police, has been driven to make this report in order to serve the Cause."

Dom Miguel looked up at me quickly, and the huge general snorted and stabbed me with his terrible eyes.

"What do you mean?" demanded Fonseca.

"This report proves, I fear, that our suspicions of Madam Izabel are well founded," I explained, not daring to look at Dom Miguel while I accused his daughter. "Paola has doubtless discovered that this information regarding the vault and its mysterious key has either been forwarded to the Emperor or is on the way to him. Therefore he has forestalled Madam Izabel's report, in order that he may prove his department vigilant in serving the government, and so protect his high office. Can you not see that Paola's claim that he is working to secure the ring is but a ruse to gain time for us? Really, he knows that he could obtain it by arresting Dom Miguel. But this report will prevent the Emperor putting his man Valcour upon the case, which he would probably have done had he received his first information from Izabel de Mar."

For a moment there was silence. Then the general's brow unbent and he said with cheerfulness:

"This explanation is entirely reasonable. It would not do for Paola to get himself deposed, or even suspected, at this juncture. A new Minister of Police would redouble our danger."

"How did you obtain this copy of the report?" asked de Pintra.

"From one of our spies."

"I have no doubt," said I, "that Paola was instrumental in sending it to you. It is a warning, gentlemen. We must not delay in acting upon it, and removing our treasure and our records to a safer place."

"And where is that?" asked Fonseca.

I looked at the chief. He sat thoughtfully considering the matter.

"There is no need of immediate haste," said he presently, "and nothing can be done tonight, in any event. Tomorrow we will pack everything in chests and carry them to Senhor Bastro, who has a safe hiding-place. Meantime, General, you may leave me your men to serve as escort. How many are there?"

"Three. They are now guarding the usual approaches to this house."

"Let them ride with you to the station at Cruz, and send them back to me in the morning. I will also summon some of our nearby patriots. By noon tomorrow everything will be ready for the transfer."

"Very good!" exclaimed the general. "We cannot abandon too soon the vault we constructed with so much care. Where is your daughter?"

"In her apartments."

"Before you leave tomorrow, lock her up and put a guard at her door. We must not let her suspect the removal of the records."

"It shall be done," answered de Pintra, with a sigh. "It may be," he continued, hesitatingly, "that my confidence in Izabel has been misplaced."

The general did not reply. He folded his cloak about him, glanced at the clock, and strode from the room without a word of farewell.

When he had gone Dom Miguel turned to me.

"Well?" said he.

"I do not like Fonseca," I answered.

"As a man he is at times rather disagreeable," admitted the chief. "But as a general he possesses rare ability, and his high station renders him the most valuable leader the Cause can boast. Moreover, Fonseca has risked everything in our enterprise, and may be implicitly trusted. When at last we strike our great blow for freedom, much will depend upon Manuel da Fonseca. And now, Robert, let us retire, for an hour before daybreak we must be at work."

It was then eleven o'clock. I bade the chief goodnight and retired to my little room next the study. Dom Miguel slept in a similar apartment opening from the opposite side of the study.

The exciting interview with Fonseca had left me nervous and wakeful, and it was sometime before I sank into a restless slumber.

A hand upon my shoulder aroused me.

It was Dom Miguel.

"Come quick, for God's sake!" he cried, in trembling tones. "She has stolen my ring!"

VIII

A Terrible Crime

S carcely awake, I sprang from my couch in time to see de Pintra's form disappear through the doorway. A moment later I was in the study, which was beginning to lighten with the dawn of a new day.

The trap in the floor was open, and the chief threw himself into the aperture and quickly descended. At once I followed, feeling my way down the iron staircase and along the passage. Reaching the domed chamber a strange sight met our view. Both traps had been raised, the second one standing upright upon its hinged edge, and from the interior of the vault shone a dim light.

While we hesitated the light grew stronger, and soon Madam Izabel came slowly from the vault with a small lamp in one hand and a great bundle of papers in the other. As she reached the chamber Dom Miguel sprang from out the shadow and wrenched the papers from her grasp.

"So, madam!" he cried, "you have betrayed yourself in seeking to betray us. Shame! Shame that a daughter of mine should be guilty of so vile an act!" As he spoke he struck her so sharply across the face with the bundle of papers that she reeled backward and almost dropped the lamp.

"Look to her, Robert," he said, and leaped into the vault to restore the papers to their place.

Then, while I stood stupidly by, not thinking of any further danger, Madam Izabel sprang to the trap and with one quick movement dashed down the heavy plate of steel. I saw her place the ring in its cavity and heard the shooting of the bolts; and then, suddenly regaining my senses, I rushed forward and seized her arm.

"The ring!" I gasped, in horror; "give me the ring! He will suffocate in that dungeon in a few minutes."

I can see yet her cold, serpent-like eyes as they glared venomously into my own. The next instant she dashed the lamp into my face. It shivered against the wall, and as I staggered backward the burning oil streamed down my pajamas and turned me into a living pillar of fire.

Screaming with pain, I tore the burning cloth from my body and stamped it into ashes with my bare feet. Then, smarting from the sting of many burns, I looked about me and found myself in darkness and alone.

Instantly the danger that menaced Dom Miguel flashed upon me anew, and I stumbled up the iron stairs until I reached the study, where I set the alarm bell going so fiercely that its deep tones resounded throughout the whole house.

In my chamber I hastily pulled my clothing over my smarting flesh, and as the astonished servants came pouring into the study, I shouted to them:

"Find Senhora de Mar immediately and bring her to me—by force if necessary. She has murdered Dom Miguel!"

Over the heads of the stupidly staring group I saw a white, startled face, and Lesba's great eyes met my own with a quick look of comprehension. Then she disappeared, and I turned again to the wondering servants.

"Make haste!" I cried. "Can you not understand? Every moment is precious."

But the frightened creatures gazed upon each other silently, and I thrust them aside and ran through the house in frantic search for the murderess. The rooms were all vacant, and when I reached the entrance hall a groom stopped me.

"Senhora de Mar left the house five minutes ago, sir. She was mounted upon our swiftest horse, and knows every inch of the country. It would be useless to pursue her."

While I glared at the fellow a soft hand touched my elbow.

"Come!" said Lesba. "Your horse is waiting—I have saddled him myself. Make for the station at Cruz, for Izabel will seek to board the train for Rio."

She had led me through the door across the broad piazza; and as, half-dazed, I mounted the horse, she added, "Tell me, can I do anything in your absence?"

"Nothing!" I cried, with a sob; "Dom Miguel is locked up in the vault, and I must find the key—the key!"

Away dashed the horse, and over my shoulder I saw her still standing on the steps of the piazza staring after me.

The station at Cruz! I must reach it as soon as possible—before Izabel de Mar should escape. Almost crazed at the thought of my impotency and shuddering at the knowledge that de Pintra was slowly dying in his tomb while I was powerless to assist him, I lashed the good steed until it fairly flew over the uneven road.

"Halt!" cried a stern voice.

The way had led me beneath some overhanging trees, and as I pulled the horse back upon his haunches I caught the gleam of a revolver held by a mounted man whose form was enveloped in a long cloak.

Then came a peal of light laughter.

"Why, 'tis our Americano!" said the horseman, gayly; "whither away, my gallant cavalier?"

To my delight I recognized Paola's voice.

"Dom Miguel is imprisoned in the vault!" I almost screamed in my agitation; "and Madam Izabel has stolen the key."

"Indeed!" he answered. "And where is Senhora Izabel?"

"She has fled to Rio."

"And left her dear father to die? How unfilial!" he retorted, laughing again. "Do you know, Senhor Harcliffe, it somehow reminds me of a story my nurse used to read me from the 'Arabian Nights,' how a fond daughter planned to—"

"For God's sake, sir, the man is dying!" I cried, maddened at his indifference.

He drew out a leathern case and calmly selected a cigarette.

"And Madam Izabel has the key," he repeated, striking a match. "By the way, senhor, where are you bound?"

"To overtake the murderess before she can board the train at Cruz."

"Very good. How long has Dom Miguel been imprisoned in the vault?"

"Twenty minutes, a half-hour, perhaps."

"Ah! He may live in that foul and confined atmosphere for two hours; possibly three. But no longer. I know, for I planned the vault myself. And the station at Cruz is a good two hours' ride from this spot. I know, for I have just traveled it."

I dropped my head, overwhelmed by despair as the truth was thus brutally thrust upon me. For Dom Miguel there was no hope.

"But the records, sir! We must save them, even if our chief is lost. Should Madam Izabel deliver the key to her husband or to the Emperor every leader of the Cause may perish upon the gallows."

"Well thought of, on my word," commented the strange man, again laughing softly. "I wonder how it feels to have a rope around one's neck and to kick the empty air?" He blew a cloud of smoke from his mouth and watched it float away. "But you are quite right, Senhor Harcliffe. The lady must be found and made to give up the ring."

He uttered a low whistle, and two men rode out from the shadow of the trees and joined us.

"Ride with Senhor Harcliffe to the station at Cruz. Take there the train for Rio. Present the American to Mazanovitch, who is to obey his instructions."

The men bowed silently.

"But you, senhor," I said, eagerly, "can you not yourself assist us in this search?"

"I never work," was the reply, drawled in his mincing manner. "But the men I have given you will do all that can be done to assist you. For myself, I think I shall ride on to de Pintra's and kiss my sister good morning. Perhaps she will give me a bite of breakfast, who knows?"

Such heartlessness amazed me. Indeed, the man was past my comprehension.

"And General Fonseca?" said I, hesitating whether or no to put myself under Paola's command, now that the chief was gone.

"Let Fonseca go to the devil. He would cry 'I told you so!' and refuse to aid you, even though his own neck is in jeopardy." He looked at his watch. "If you delay longer you will miss the train at Cruz. Good morning, senhor. How sad that you cannot breakfast with us!"

Touching his hat with a gesture of mock courtesy he rode slowly on, and the next moment, all irresolution vanishing, I put spurs to my horse and bounded away, the two men following at my heels.

Presently I became tortured with thoughts of Dom Miguel, stifling in his tomb of steel. And under my breath I cursed the heartless *sang froid* of Francisco Paola, who refused to be serious even when his friend was dying.

"The cold-blooded scoundrel!" I muttered, as I galloped on; "the cad! the trifling coxcomb! Can nothing rouse him from his self-complaisant idiocy?"

"I imagine you are apostrophizing my master, senhor," said one of the men riding beside me.

Something in his voice caused me to turn and scrutinize his face.

"Ah!" I exclaimed, "you are Sergeant Marco."

"The same, senhor. And I shall not arrest you for the death of our dear lieutenant." A low chuckling laugh accompanied the grim pleasantry. "But if you were applying those sweet names to Senhor Paola, I assure you that you wrong him. For three years I have been his servant, and this I have learned: in an emergency no man can think more clearly or act more swiftly than his Majesty's Minister of Police."

"I have been with him four years," announced the other man, in a hoarse voice, "and I agree with you that he is cold and heartless. Yet I never question the wisdom of his acts."

"Why did he not come with us himself?" I demanded, angrily. "Why should he linger to eat a breakfast and kiss his sister good morning, when his friend and chief is dying, and his Cause is in imminent danger?"

Marco laughed, and the other shrugged his shoulders, disdaining a reply.

For a time we rode on in unbroken silence, but coming to a rough bit of road that obliged us to walk the horses, the sergeant said:

"Perhaps it would be well for you to explain to us what has happened. My friend Figgot, here, is a bit of a detective, and if we are to assist you we must know in what way our services are required."

"We are both patriots, senhor," said the other, briefly.

So I told them the story of Madam Izabel's treachery and her theft of the ring, after locking her father within the vault. At their request I explained minutely the construction of the steel doors and described the cutting of the emerald that alone could release the powerful bolts. They heard all without comment, and how much of my story was new to them I had no knowledge. But of one thing I felt certain: these fellows were loyal to the Cause and clever enough to be chosen by Paola as his especial companions; therefore they were just the assistants I needed in this emergency.

It was a weary ride, and the roads became worse as we progressed toward Cruz. The sun had risen and now spread a marvelous radiance over the tropical landscape. I noted the beauty of the morning even while smarting from the burns upon my breast and arms, and heart-sick at the awful fate of my beloved leader—even now perishing amid the records of the great conspiracy he had guided so successfully. Was all over yet, I wondered? Paola had said that he might live in his prison for two or three hours. And the limit of time had nearly passed. Poor Dom Miguel!

My horse stepped into a hole, stumbled, and threw me headlong to the ground.

For a few minutes I was unconscious; then I found myself sitting up and supported by Sergeant Marco, while the other man dashed water in my face.

"It is a dangerous delay," grumbled Marco, seeing me recovering.

Slowly I rose to my feet. No bones were broken, but I was sadly bruised.

"I can ride, now," I said.

They lifted me upon one of their horses and together mounted the other. My own steed had broken his leg. A bullet ended his suffering.

Another half-hour and we sighted the little station at Cruz. Perhaps I should have explained before that from Cuyaba to Cruz the railway made a long sweep around the base of the hills. The station nearest to de Pintra's estate was Cuyaba; but by riding straight to Cruz one saved nearly an hour's railway journey, and the train for Rio could often be made in this way when it was impossible to reach Cuyaba in time to intercept it. And as the station at Cruz was more isolated than that at Cuyaba, this route was greatly preferred by the revolutionists visiting de Pintra.

My object in riding to Cruz upon this occasion was twofold. Had Madam Izabel in her flight made for Cuyaba to catch the train, I should be able to board the same train at Cruz, and force her to give up the ring. And if she rode to Cruz she must await there the coming of the train we also hoped to meet. In either event I planned, as soon as the ring was in my possession, to hasten back to the mansion, open the vault and remove the body of our chief; after which it would be my duty to convey the records and treasure to the safe-keeping of Senhor Bastro.

I had no expectation of finding Dom Miguel still alive. With everything in our favor the trip would require five hours, and long before that time the prisoner's fate would have overtaken him. But the chief's dying wish would be to save the records, and that I intended to do if it were possible.

However, the delays caused by meeting with Paola and my subsequent unlucky fall had been fatal to my plans. We dashed up to the Cruz station in time to see the train for Rio disappearing in the distance, and to complete my disappointment we found standing beside the platform a horse yet panting and covered with foam.

Quickly dismounting, I approached the horse to examine it. The station master came from his little house and bowed with native politeness.

"The horse? Ah, yes; it was from the stables of Dom Miguel. Senhora de Mar had arrived upon the animal just in time to take the express for Rio. The gentleman also wanted the train? How sad to have missed it! But there would be another at eleven o'clock, although not so fast a train."

For a time I stood in a sort of stupor, my mind refusing to grasp the full horror of the situation. Until then, perhaps, a lingering hope of saving Dom Miguel had possessed me. But with the ring on its way to

Rio and the Emperor, and I condemned to inaction at a deserted way-station, it is no wonder that despair overwhelmed me.

When I slowly recovered my faculties I found that my men and the station master had disappeared. I found them in the little house writing telegrams, which the official was busily ticking over the wires.

Glancing at one or two of the messages I found them unintelligible.

"It is the secret cypher," whispered Figgot. "We shall put Madam Izabel in the care of Mazanovitch himself. Ah, how he will cling to the dear lady! She is clever—ah, yes! exceedingly clever is Senhora de Mar. But has Mazanovitch his match in all Brazil?"

"I do not know the gentleman," I returned.

"No? Perhaps not. But you know the Minister of Police, and Mazanovitch is the soul of Francisco Paola."

"But what are we to do?" I asked, impatiently.

"Why, now that our friends in Rio are informed of the situation, we have transferred to them, for a time, all our worries. It only remains for us to await the eleven o'clock train."

I nodded, staring at him through a sort of haze. I was dimly conscious that my burns were paining me terribly and that my right side seemed pierced by a thousand red-hot needles. Then the daylight faded away, the room grew black, and I sank upon the floor unconscious.

IX

The Missing Finger

When I recovered I was lying upon a cot in the station-master's private room. Sergeant Marco had ridden to a neighboring farmhouse and procured bandages and some olive oil and Figgot, who proudly informed me he had once been a surgeon, had neatly dressed and bandaged my burns.

These now bothered me less than the lameness resulting from my fall; but I drank a glass of wine and then lay quietly upon the cot until the arrival of the train, when my companions aroused me and assisted me aboard.

I made the journey comfortably enough, and felt greatly refreshed after partaking of a substantial luncheon brought from an eating-house by the thoughtful Figgot.

On our arrival at Rio we were met by a little, thin-faced man who thrust us all three into a cab and himself joined us as we began to rattle along the labyrinth of streets. He was plainly dressed in black, quiet and unobtrusive in manner, and had iron-gray hair and beard, both closely cropped. I saw at once he was not a Brazilian, and made up my mind he was the man called Mazanovitch by Paola and my companions. If so, he was the person now in charge of our quest for the ring, and with this idea I examined his face with interest.

This was not difficult, for the man sat opposite me with lowered eyelids and a look of perfect repose upon his thin features. He might have been fifty or sixty years of age; but there was no guide in determining this except his gray hairs, for his face bore no lines of any sort, and his complexion, although of pallid hue, was not unhealthy in appearance.

It surprised me that neither he nor my companions asked any questions. Perhaps the telegrams had explained all that was necessary. Anyway, an absolute silence reigned in the carriage during our brief drive.

When we came to a stop the little man opened the door. We all alighted and followed him into a gloomy stone building. Through several passages we walked, and then our conductor led us into a small chamber, bare except for a half-dozen iron cots that stood in a row against the wall. A guard was at the doorway, but admitted us with a low bow after one glance at the man in black.

Leading us to the nearest cot, Mazanovitch threw back a sheet and then stood aside while we crowded around it. To my horror I saw the form of Madam Izabel lying dead before us. Her white dress was discolored at the breast with clots of dark blood.

"Stabbed to the heart," said the guard, calmly. "It was thus they brought her from the train that arrived this afternoon from Matto Grosso. The assassin is unknown."

Mazanovitch thrust me aside, leaned over the cot, and drew the woman's left hand from beneath the sheet.

The little finger had been completely severed.

Very gently he replaced the hand, drew the sheet over the beautiful face, and turned away.

Filled with amazement at the Nemesis that had so soon overtaken this fierce and terrible woman, I was about to follow our guide when I found myself confronting a personage who stood barring my way with folded arms and a smile of grim satisfaction upon his delicate features.

It was Valcour—the man who had called himself de Guarde on board the Castina—the Emperor's spy.

"Ah, my dear Senhor Harcliffe! Do we indeed meet again?" he cried, tauntingly. "And are you still keeping a faithful record in that sweet diary of yours? It is fine reading, that diary—perhaps you have it with you now?"

"Let me pass," said I, impatiently.

"Not yet, my dear friend," he answered, laughing. "You are going to be my guest, you know. Will it not please you to enjoy my society once more? To be sure. And I—I shall not wish to part with you again soon."

"What do you mean?" I demanded.

"Only that I arrest you, Robert Harcliffe, in the name of the Emperor!"

"On what charge?" I asked.

"Murder, for one," returned the smiling Valcour. "Afterward you may answer for conspiracy."

"Pardon me, Senhor Valcour," said the little man, in a soft voice. "The gentleman is already under arrest—in the Emperor's name."

Valcour turned upon him fiercely, but his eyes fell as he encountered the other's passive, unemotional countenance.

"Is it so, Captain Mazanovitch? Then I will take the prisoner off your hands."

The little man spread out his palms with an apologetic, deprecating gesture. His eyes seemed closed—or nearly so. He seemed to see nothing; he looked at neither Valcour nor myself. But there was something about the still, white face, with its frame of iron-gray, that compelled a certain respect, and even deference.

"It is greatly to be regretted," he said, gently; "and it grieves me to be obliged to disappoint you, Senhor Valcour. But since this man is a prisoner of the police—a state prisoner of some importance, I believe—it is impossible to deliver him into your hands."

Without answer Valcour stood motionless before us, only his mobile face and his white lips showing the conflict of emotions that oppressed him. And then I saw a curious thing happen. The eyelids of Mazanovitch for an instant unclosed, and in that instant so tender a glance escaped them that Valcour trembled slightly, and touched with a gentle, loving gesture the elder man's arm.

It all happened in a flash, and the next moment I could not have sworn that my eyes had not deceived me, for Valcour turned away with a sullen frown upon his brow, and the Captain seized my arm and marched me to the door, Figgot and Marco following close behind.

Presently we regained our carriage and were driven rapidly from the morgue.

This drive was longer than the first, but during it no word was spoken by any of my companions. I could not help staring at the closed eyes of Mazanovitch, but the others, I noticed, avoided looking at him. Did he see, I wondered?—*could* he see from out the tiny slit that showed beneath his lashes?

We came at last to a quiet street lined with small frame houses, and before one of these the carriage stopped. Mazanovitch opened the front door with a latchkey, and ushered us into a dimly lighted room that seemed fitted up as study and office combined.

Not until we were seated and supplied with cigars did the little man speak. Then he reclined in a cushioned chair, puffed at his cheroot, and turned his face in my direction.

"Tell me all you know concerning the vault and the ring which unlocks it," he said, in his soft tones.

I obeyed. Afterward Figgot told of my meeting with the Minister of Police, and of Paola's orders to him and Marco to escort me to Rio and to place the entire matter in the hands of Mazanovitch.

The little man listened without comment and afterward sat for many minutes silently smoking his cheroot.

"It seems to me," said I, at last, "that the death of Senhora de Mar, and especially the fact that her ring finger has been severed from her hand, points conclusively to one reassuring fact; that the ring has been recovered by one of our band, and so the Cause is no longer endangered. Therefore my mission to Rio is ended, and all that remains for me is to return to Cuyaba and attend to the obsequies of my poor friend de Pintra."

Marco and Figgot heard me respectfully, but instead of replying both gazed questioningly at the calm face of Mazanovitch.

"The facts are these"; said the latter, deliberately; "Senhora de Mar fled with the ring; she has been murdered, and the ring taken from her. By whom? If a patriot has it we shall know the truth within fifteen minutes." I glanced at a great clock ticking against the wall. "Before your arrival," he resumed, "I had taken steps to communicate with every patriot in Rio. Yet there were few able to recognize the ring as the key to the secret vault, and the murder was committed fifteen minutes after the train left Cruz."

I started, at that.

"Who could have known?" I asked.

The little man took the cigar from his mouth for a moment.

"On the train," said he, "were General Fonseca, the patriot, and Senhor Valcour, the Emperor's spy."

X

"For Tomorrow We Die!"

I remembered Fonseca's visit of the night before, and considered it natural he should take the morning train to the capital.

"But Valcour would not need to murder Madam Izabel," said I. "They were doubtless in the plot together, and she would have no hesitation in giving him the ring had he demanded it. On the contrary, our general was already incensed against the daughter of the chief, and suspected her of plotting mischief. I am satisfied he has the ring."

"The general will be with us presently," answered Mazanovitch, quietly. "But, gentlemen, you all stand in need of refreshment, and Senhor Harcliffe should have his burns properly dressed. Kindly follow me."

He led the way up a narrow flight of stairs that made two abrupt turns—for no apparent reason—before they reached the upper landing. Following our guide we came to a back room where a table was set for six. A tall, studious-looking Brazilian greeted us with a bow and immediately turned his spectacled eyes upon me. On a small side table were bandages, ointments, and a case of instruments lying open.

Within ten minutes the surgeon had dressed all my wounds—none of which, however, was serious, merely uncomfortable—and I felt greatly benefited by the application of the soothing ointments.

Scarcely was the operation completed when the door opened to admit Fonseca. He gave me a nod, glanced questioningly at the others, and then approached the table and poured out a glass of wine, which he drank eagerly. I noticed he was in full uniform.

"General," said I, unable to repress my anxiety, "have you the ring?"

He shook his head and sat down with a gloomy expression upon his face.

"I slept during the journey from Cuyaba," he said presently, "and only on my arrival at Rio did I discover that Senhora de Mar had traveled by the same train. She was dead when they carried her into the station."

"And Valcour?" It was Mazanovitch who asked the question.

"Valcour was beside the body, wild with excitement, and swearing vengeance against the murderer."

"Be seated, gentlemen," requested our host, approaching the table. "We have time for a slight repast before our friends arrive."

"May I join you?" asked a high, querulous voice. A slender figure, draped in black and slightly stooping, stood in the doorway.

"Come in," said Fonseca, and the new arrival threw aside his cloak and sat with us at the table.

"The last supper, eh?" he said, in a voice that quavered somewhat. "For tomorrow we die. Eh, brothers?—tomorrow we die!"

"Croaker!" cried Fonseca, with scorn. "Die tomorrow, if you like; die tonight, for all I care. The rest of us intend to live long enough to shout huzzas for the United States of Brazil!"

"In truth, Senhor Piexoto," said Marco, who was busily eating, "we are in no unusual danger tonight."

Startled by the mention of the man's name, I regarded him with sudden interest.

The reputation of Floriano Piexoto, the astute statesman who had plotted so well for the revolutionary party, was not unknown to me, by any means. Next to Fonseca no patriot was more revered by the people of Brazil; yet not even the general was regarded with the same unquestioning affection. For Piexoto was undoubtedly a friend of the people, and despite his personal peculiarities had the full confidence of that rank and file of the revolutionary party upon which, more than upon the grandees who led it, depended the fate of the rising republic.

His smooth-shaven face, sunken cheeks, and somewhat deprecating gaze gave him the expression of a student rather than a statesman, and his entire personality was in sharp contrast to the bravado of Fonseca. To see the two leaders together one would never suspect that history would prove the statesman greater than the general.

"Danger!" piped Piexoto, shrilly, in answer to Sergeant Marco's remark, "you say there is no danger? Is not de Pintra dead? Is not the ring gone? Is not the secret vault at the Emperor's mercy?"

"Who knows?" answered Fonseca, with a shrug.

"And who is this?" continued Piexoto, turning upon me a penetrating gaze. "Ah, the American secretary, I suppose. Well, sir, what excuse have you to make for allowing all this to happen under your very nose? Are you also a traitor?"

"I have not the honor of your acquaintance, senhor," said I, stiffly; "nor, in view of your childish conduct, do I greatly desire it."

Fonseca laughed, and the Pole turned his impassive face, with its half-closed eyelids, in my direction. But Piexoto seemed rather pleased with my retort, and said:

"Never mind; your head sits as insecurely upon its neck as any present. 'Tis really a time for action rather than recrimination. What do you propose, Mazanovitch?"

"I am waiting to hear if you have discovered the present possessor of the ring," answered the captain.

"No; our people were ignorant of its very existence, save in a few cases, and none of them has seen it. Therefore the Emperor has it, without doubt."

"Why without doubt?" asked Mazanovitch.

"Who else could desire it? Who else could know its value? Who else would have murdered Madam Izabel to secure it?"

"Why the devil should the Emperor cause his own spy to be murdered?" inquired Fonseca, in his harsh voice. "You are a fool, Piexoto."

"What of Leon de Mar?" asked the other, calmly. "He hated his wife. Why should he not have killed her himself, in order to be rid of her and at the same time secure the honor of presenting his Emperor with the key to the secret vault?"

"Leon de Mar," said Mazanovitch, "is in Rio Grande do Sul. He has been stationed there for three weeks."

For a time there was silence.

"Where is Paola?" suddenly asked Piexoto. "I want to know what Paola is doing in this crisis."

"He was last seen near de Pintra's residence," said Figgot. "But we know nothing of his present whereabouts."

"You may be sure of one thing," declared Marco stoutly; "that Francisco Paola is serving the Cause, wherever he may be."

The general snorted derisively, and Piexoto looked at him with the nearest approach to a smile his anxious face had shown.

"How we admire one another!" he murmured.

"Personally I detest both you and Paola," responded the general, frankly. "But the Cause is above personalities, and as for your loyalty, I dare not doubt it. But we wander from the subject in hand. Has the Emperor the ring or is he seeking it as eagerly as we are?"

"The Emperor has not the ring," said Mazanovitch, slowly; "you may be assured of that. Otherwise—"

Piexoto gave a start.

"To be sure," said he, "otherwise we would not be sitting here."

XI

Lesba's Bright Eyes

Later that evening there was a large gathering of the important members of the conspiracy, but the result of their deliberations only served to mystify us more than before as to the murderer of Madam Izabel and the possessor of the ring. Many were the expressions of sorrow at the terrible fate of Dom Miguel—a man beloved by all who had known him. The sad incident of his death caused several to waver in their loyalty to the projected Republic, and I was impressed by the fact that at this juncture the Cause seemed to be in rather desperate straits.

"If the ring is gone and the records discovered," said one, "we would best leave the country for a time, until the excitement subsides, for the Emperor will spare no one in his desire for vengeance."

"Let us first wait for more definite information," counseled the old general, always optimistic. "Should an uprising be precipitated at this time we have all the advantage on our side, for the Republic is today stronger than the Empire. And we have yet to hear from Paola."

So, after much comment, it was determined to watch every action of the court party with redoubled vigilance, and in case danger threatened the republicans, to give the signal that would set the revolution going in full swing. Meantime we would endeavor to get in touch with Paola.

But the Minister of Police had mysteriously disappeared, and although telegrams were sent in every direction, we could hear nothing of Paola's whereabouts. Inquiries at the court failed to elicit any information whatever, and they were doubtless as ignorant on the subject as ourselves.

Officially, I was supposed to be occupying a dungeon in the fortress, and Mazanovitch had actually locked up a man under my name, registering the prisoner in the prescribed fashion. Therefore, being cleverly disguised by the detective, I ran little risk of interference should I venture abroad in the city.

Curiously enough, Mazanovitch chose to disguise me as a member of the police, saying that this plan was less likely than any other to lead to discovery. Wherever I might wander I was supposed to be off duty or on special service, and the captain enrolled me under the name of Andrea Subig.

I was anxious at times to return to Cuyaba, for Lesba's white face, as I had last seen it on the morning of Dom Miguel's incarceration, haunted me perpetually. But the quest of the ring was of vital importance, and I felt that I dared not return until I could remove my dear friend's body from the vault and see it properly interred.

Under Mazanovitch's directions I strove earnestly to obtain a clue that might lead to a knowledge of where the missing ring was secreted; but our efforts met with no encouragement, and we were not even sure that the murderer of Izabel de Mar had ever reached the capital.

On the third morning after my arrival I was strolling down the street toward the railway station, in company with Mazanovitch, when suddenly I paused and grasped my comrade's arm convulsively.

"Look there!" I exclaimed.

Mazanovitch shook off my hand, impatiently.

"I see," he returned; "it is the Senhorita Lesba Paola, riding in the Emperor's carriage."

"But that scoundrel Valcour is with her!" I cried.

"Scoundrel? We do not call Senhor Valcour that. He is faithful to the Emperor, who employs him. Shall we, who are unfaithful, blame him for his fidelity?"

While I sought an answer to this disconcerting query the carriage whirled past us and disappeared around a corner; but I had caught a glimpse of Lesba's bright eyes glancing coyly into the earnest face Valcour bent over her, and the sight filled me with pain and suspicion.

"Listen, Captain," said I, gloomily, "that girl knows all the important secrets of the conspiracy."

"True," answered the unmoved Mazanovitch.

"And she is riding in the Emperor's carriage, in confidential intercourse with the Emperor's spy."

"True," he said again.

"Paola has disappeared, and his sister is at court. What do you make of it, senhor?"

"Pardon me, the Minister of Police returned to his duties this morning," said the man, calmly. "Doubtless his sister accompanied him. Who knows?"

"Why did you not tell me this?" I demanded, angrily.

"I am waiting for Paola to communicate with us, which he will do in good time. Meanwhile, let me counsel patience, Senhor Americano."

But I left him and strode down the street, very impatient indeed, and filled with strange misgivings. These Brazilians were hard to understand, and were it not for Lesba I could wish myself quit of their country forever.

Lesba? What strange chance had brought her to Rio and thrown her into the companionship of the man most inimical to her brother, to myself, and to the Cause?

Was she playing a double game? Could this frank, clear-eyed girl be a traitor to the Republic, as had been Izabel de Mar?

It might be. A woman's mind is hard to comprehend. But she had been so earnest a patriot, so sincerely interested in our every success, so despondent over our disappointments, that even now I could not really doubt her faith.

Moreover, I loved the girl. Had I never before realized the fact, I knew it in this hour when she seemed lost to me forever. For never had speech of mine brought the glad look to her face that I had noted as she flashed by with Valcour pouring soft speeches into her ears. The Emperor's spy was a handsome fellow; he was high in favor at court; he was one of her own people—

Was he, by the by? Was Valcour really a Brazilian? He had a Brazilian's dark eyes and complexion, it is true; yet now that I thought upon it, there was an odd, foreign cast to his features that indicated he belonged to another race. Yes, there was a similarity between them and the features of the Pole Mazanovitch. Perhaps Valcour might also be a Pole. Just now Mazanovitch had spoken kindly of him, and—

I stopped short in my calculations, for I had made a second startling discovery. My wanderings had led me to the railway station, where, as I approached, I saw the Emperor of Brazil, Dom Pedro de Alcantara, surrounded by a company of his Uruguayan guard, and in the act of boarding a private car attached to the Matto Grosso train.

I had never before seen the Emperor, but from descriptions of him, as well as from the deference of those about him, I had no doubt of his identity.

His hurried departure upon a journey, coupled with Paola's presence at the capital, could only bear one interpretation. The Minister of Police had been in conference with the Emperor, and his Majesty was about to visit in person the scene of the late tragedy, and do what he might to unearth the records of that far-reaching revolution which threatened his throne.

Here was news, indeed! Half-dazed, I started to retrace my steps, when a soft voice beside me said:

"Have you money, senhor?"

"Yes," I answered.

"Then," continued Mazanovitch, "you must take this train for Cuyaba. Let the Emperor guide you. If danger threatens us, telegraph me the one word, 'Lesba'! Do you understand, Senhor Harcliffe?"

"I think so," said I, "but let me use someother word. Why drag a woman's name into this affair?"

He coughed slightly.

"It is a word you will remember," said he. "Good by to you, senhor."

He had an odd way of disappearing, this strange Pole, whose eyes I had never seen. With his last word he actually melted into the crowd of loiterers who were watching the Emperor's departure, and I could not have found him again had I so desired.

My first thought was to rebel at leaving Rio, where Lesba Paola had taken refuge from the coming storm. But the girl seemed amply amused without me, and my duties to the interests of my dead chieftain forbade my deserting the Cause at this crisis. Therefore I would follow the Emperor.

As the train moved slowly out of the station, I swung myself upon the steps of the rear car, and the next instant was tumbled upon the platform by a person who sprang up behind me.

Angrily protesting, I scrambled to my feet; but the fellow, with scarcely a glance in my direction, passed into the car and made his way forward.

The exclamations died suddenly upon my lips.

The belated passenger was Senhor Valcour, the spy.

XII

The Man in the Shrubbery

The name of an Emperor is a fine thing to conjure with. When we arrived at the station at Cuyaba at early evening a score of saddle-horses and several carriages were awaiting the royal party.

I stood in the shadows of the station and watched the guardsmen mount and surround the equipage in which their imperial master seated himself. His civic companions—men of high rank, evidently—occupied the other carriages; and then the entire cavalcade swept away into the gloom and left me alone.

The station agent was known to me as a patriot, but he was still bobbing his head after the royal party when I accosted him.

"Get me a horse, Pedro."

"A horse! Ah, your excellency is joking. Every horse that could be found has been impressed by the Emperor."

"Anything will do. A nag of any sort, with saddle or cart, will answer my purpose. The Cause demands it, Pedro."

"I am powerless, your excellency. Absolutely powerless!"

It was true enough. The only way for me to get to de Pintra's mansion was on foot, and after inducing the man to give me a peasant's dress in exchange for my police uniform, I set out at once.

It was a long and gloomy walk. There was a moon, but large banks of clouds were drifting across the sky, and the way was obscured more than half the time, causing me to go slowly in order to avoid stumbling into the ditches.

I met no one on the road, for the highways were usually deserted at this hour, and the silence all about me added its depressing influence to the anxiety of my thoughts.

The Emperor's advent into this stronghold of the Revolution indicated that at last he had determined to act and suppress the conspiracy that had grown to such huge proportions. With the real leader—"the brains of the revolt," as de Pintra was called—out of the way, Dom Pedro doubtless had concluded he could easily crush the remainder of the conspirators.

But his success, I argued, would depend upon his securing the key to the secret vault, for without that the records would never come into his possession.

Did he have the key? Was this the explanation of his sudden activity? The thought made me hasten my steps, but although I put forth my best efforts it was close upon midnight before I sighted the great hedge that surrounded de Pintra's mansion. I half-expected to find the gateway guarded, but to my relief the avenue was as deserted as the highway had been.

Cautiously I passed along the drive leading to the mansion. I am not usually nervous at such times, but something in the absolute stillness of the scene, something menacing in the deep shadows cast by the great trees, unnerved me and made me suspicious of my surrounding.

Once, indeed, I fancied that I heard a stealthy footstep advancing to meet me, and with a bound I sprang from the driveway and crouched among the thick shrubbery, listening intently. But after a few moments I became reassured and resumed my journey, avoiding this time the graveled drive and picking my way noiselessly across the grass, skirting the endless array of flower-beds and shrubbery.

Fortunately the moon came out, or I might have lost my way; and before long the black line of shadow cast by the mansion itself fell at my feet. Peering ahead, I saw that I had approached the right wing of the house. It was here that my own room was located, and with a low exclamation of relief I was about to step forward into the path when my eyes fell upon a sight that caused me to suddenly halt and recoil in horror.

It was a man's arm showing white in the moonlight, and extending from beneath a clump of low bushes.

For a few moments I gazed at it as if fascinated, but quickly recovering myself I advanced to the bushes and gently withdrew the body until it lay exposed to the full rays of the moon. I fully expected to recognize one of our conspirators, but when I turned the man over a face was disclosed that was wholly unknown to me—that of a dark, swarthy person of evident intelligence and refinement.

He had been shot squarely between the eyes, and doubtless had met death instantly. I was about to consider the man a government spy who had been killed by Paola or someother of the conspirators, when I discovered, with a start of dismay, that the man's left hand had been completely severed at the wrist. Also the hand was missing, and although I searched the ground carefully in the neighborhood, I could find no trace of it.

This discovery gave me ample food for thought. The only plausible reason for the hasty amputation of the hand had doubtless been to secure a ring which the dead man had worn—the secret key to Dom Miguel's vault probably, since the murder had been committed at this place.

In whose possession, then, was the ring now? Madam Izabel, the Emperor's spy, had first stolen it. Then another had murdered her for its possession—not a conspirator, for all had denied any knowledge of the ring. Could it have been the man who now lay dead before me? And, if so, who was he? And had the government again managed to secure the precious jewel and to revenge Madam Izabel's assassination by mutilating this victim in the same way that she had been served?

But if the dead man was not one of the few leaders of the conspiracy who knew the secret of the ring, how should he have learned its value, and risked his life to obtain it from Madam Izabel?

That, however, was of no vital importance. The main thing was that the ring had been taken from him, and had once more changed ownership.

Perhaps Paola, lurking near his uncle's mansion, had encountered this person and killed him to get the ring. If so, had he carried it to the Emperor? And was this the explanation of Dom Pedro's sudden visit to de Pintra's residence?

Yet what object could Paola have in betraying the conspiracy at this juncture?

Filled with these thoughts I was about to proceed to the house, when a sudden thought induced me to stoop and feel of the murdered man's arm. *The flesh was still warm!*

The murder had been done that very evening—perhaps within the hour.

I own that the horror of the thing and the reckless disregard of life evinced in this double murder for the possession of the ring, warned me against proceeding further in the matter; and for the moment I had serious thoughts of returning quietly to Rio and taking the first steamer for New Orleans. But there were reasons for remaining. One was to get possession in some way of Dom Miguel's body and see it decently buried; for he was my uncle's friend, as well as my own, and I could not honorably return home and admit that I had left him lying within the dungeon where his doom had overtaken him. The second reason I could not have definitely explained. Perhaps it was curiosity to see the adventure to the end, or a secret hope that the revolution was too powerful to be balked. And then there was Lesba! At any rate, I resolved not to desert the Cause just yet, although acknowledging it to be the wisest and safest course to pursue.

So, summoning all my resolution and courage to my aid, I crept to the window of my room and, by a method that I had many times before made use of, admitted myself to the apartment.

I had seen no lights whatever shining from the windows, and the house—as I stood still and listened—seemed absolutely deserted. I felt my way to a shelf, found a candle, and lighted it.

Then I turned around and faced the barrel of a revolver that was held on a level with my eyes.

"You are our prisoner, senhor!" said a voice, stern but suppressed. "I beg you to offer no resistance."

XIII

Dom Pedro De Alcantara

I held the candle steadily and stared at my captor. He was dressed in the uniform of an officer of the royal guards—the body commanded by Fonseca. At his back were two others, silent but alert.

"You are here in the service of General da Fonseca?" I asked, with assumed composure.

"In the Emperor's service, senhor," answered the officer, quietly.

"But the general—"

"The general is unaware of our mission. I have my orders from his Majesty in person."

He smiled somewhat unpleasantly as he made this statement, and for the first time I realized that my arrest might prove a great misfortune.

"Pardon me if I appear discourteous," he continued, and made a sign to his men.

One took the candle from my hand and the other snapped a pair of hand-cuffs over my wrists.

I had no spirit to resist. The surprise had been so complete that it well-nigh benumbed my faculties. I heard the officer's voice imploring me in polite tones to follow, and then my captors extinguished the candle and marched me away through a succession of black passages until we had reached an upper room at the back of the house.

Here a door quickly opened and I was thrust into a blaze of light so brilliant that it nearly blinded me.

Blinking my eyes to accustom them to the glare, I presently began to note my surroundings, and found myself standing before a table at which was seated the Emperor of Brazil.

Involuntarily I bowed before his Majesty. He was a large man, of commanding appearance, with dark eyes that seemed to read one through and through. Behind him stood a group of four men in civilian attire, while the other end of the room was occupied by a squad of a dozen soldiers of the Uruguayan guard.

"A prisoner, your Majesty," said the officer, saluting. "One evidently familiar with the house, for he obtained entrance to a room adjoining Dom Miguel's library."

The Emperor turned from the papers that littered the table and eyed me gravely.

"Your name!" said he, in a stern voice.

I hesitated; but remembering that officially I was occupying a dungeon in Rio I decided to continue the deception of my present disguise.

"Andrea Subig, your Majesty."

Someone laughed softly beside me. I turned and saw Valcour at my elbow.

"It is the American secretary, your Majesty, one Robert Harcliffe by name."

The spy spoke in his womanish, dainty manner, and with such evident satisfaction that I could have strangled him with much pleasure had I been free.

"Why are you here?" inquired the Emperor, after eyeing me curiously for a moment.

"I have some personal belongings in this house which I wished to secure before returning to the United States. Your men arrested me in the room I have been occupying."

"Why are you anxious to return to the United States?" questioned the Emperor.

"Because my mission to Brazil is ended."

"It is true," returned Dom Pedro, positively. "The conspiracy is at an end."

"Of that I am not informed," I replied evasively. "But I have been employed by Dom Miguel de Pintra, not by the conspiracy, as your Majesty terms it. And Dom Miguel has no further need of me."

"Dom Miguel is dead," retorted the Emperor, with an accent of triumph in his voice.

"Murdered by his daughter, your spy," I added, seeing that he was aware of the truth.

He merely shrugged his broad shoulders and turned to whisper to a gray-bearded man behind him.

"This conspiracy must be summarily dealt with," resumed the Emperor, turning to me again, "and as there is ample evidence that you are guilty of treason, Senhor Harcliffe, I shall order you put to death unless you at once agree to give us such information as may be in your possession."

"I am an American citizen and entitled to a fair trial," I answered, boldly enough. "You dare not assassinate me. For if I am injured in anyway the United States will call you to full account."

"It is a matter of treason, sir!" returned the Emperor, harshly. "Your citizenship will not protect you in this case. I have myself visited your country and been received there with great courtesy. And no one knows better than I that your countrymen would repudiate one who came to Brazil for the treasonable purpose of dethroning its legitimate Emperor."

That was true enough, and I remained silent.

"Will you give us the required information?" he demanded.

I was curious to know how much the royalists had learned, and in what position the republicans had been placed by this imperial visit to their headquarters. Dom Pedro had said that the conspiracy was at an end; but I did not believe that.

"I am sure you err in believing me to be in the secret counsels of the republicans," I said, after a moment's thought. "I was merely employed in the capacity of private secretary to Dom Miguel."

"But you know of the underground vault? You have visited it?"

"Often," I replied, seeing no harm in the acknowledgment.

"Can you open it for us?" he demanded. I laughed, for the question exposed to me his real weakness.

"Your Majesty must be well aware that there is but one key," I replied, "and without that secret key I am as powerless as you are to open the vault."

"Where is the key?" he asked.

"I do not know. Senhora de Mar stole it from Dom Miguel."

"And it was taken from her by one of your conspirators."

"Have you traced it no farther?" I inquired, carelessly.

He shifted uneasily in his chair.

"My men are now investigating the matter," said he. "Doubtless the ring will soon be in our possession."

"And how about the murdered man in the shrubbery?" I asked.

The royalists exchanged glances, and one or two uttered exclamations of surprise.

"Is there a murdered man in the shrubbery, Captain de Souza?" questioned the Emperor, sternly.

"Not that I know of, your Majesty," returned the officer.

"I found him as I approached the house," said I. "He has been shot within the hour, and his left hand severed at the wrist."

It was evident that my news startled them. When I had described the location of the body some of the soldiers were sent to fetch it, and during their absence the Emperor resumed his questioning. I told him frankly that none of the records of the republicans was in my possession, and that whatever knowledge I had gained of the conspiracy or the conspirators could not be drawn from me by his threats of death. For now I began to understand that this visit to Dom Miguel's house was a secret one, and that the royalists were as much in the dark as ever regarding the conspiracy itself or the whereabouts of its leaders. One thing only they knew—that the records were lying with Dom Miguel's dead body in the secret vault, and that the ring which opened it was missing.

Before long the soldiers bore the body of the latest victim of the fatal ring into the presence of the Emperor, and Valcour bent over it eagerly for a moment, and then shook his head.

"The man is a stranger," he said.

Others present endeavored to identify the murdered man, but were equally unsuccessful.

I could see by their uneasy looks that they were all suspicious of one another; for Captain de Souza protested that no shot could have been fired without some of his men hearing it, and the fact that the ring they sought had been so recently within their very reach led them to believe it might not now be very far away.

For all the Emperor's assumed calmness, I knew he was greatly disturbed by this last murder, as well as by the impotency of his spies to discover the whereabouts of the ring. When Valcour suggested, in his soft voice, that I had myself killed the fellow in the shrubbery, and had either secreted the ring or had it now in my possession, they pounced upon me eagerly, and I was subjected to a thorough search and afterward to severe questioning and many fierce threats.

For a few moments the Emperor listened to the counsels of the group of advisors that stood at his back, and then ordered me safely confined until he had further use for me.

The officer therefore marched me away to the front of the house, where, still securely hand-cuffed, I was thrust into a small chamber and left alone. The key was turned in the lock and I heard the soft foot-falls of a guard pacing up and down outside the door.

The long walk from the station and the excitement of the last hour had greatly wearied me; so I groped around in the dark until I found the bed with which the room was provided, and soon had forgotten all about the dreary conspiracy in a refreshing sleep.

XIV

The Man with the Ring

Toward morning a tramping of feet aroused me; the door was thrust open long enough for another prisoner to be admitted, and then I heard the bolts shoot into their fastening and the soldiers march away.

It was not quite dark in the room, for the shutters were open and admitted a ray of moonlight through the window. So I lay still and strained my eyes to discover who my companion might be.

He stood motionless for a time in the place the soldiers had left him. I made out that he was tall and stooping, and exceedingly thin; but his face was in shadow. Presently, as he moved, I heard a chain clank, and knew he was hand-cuffed in the same manner as myself.

Slowly he turned his body, peering into every corner of the room, so that soon he discovered me lying where the moonlight was strongest. He gave a start, then, but spoke no word; and again an interval of absolute silence ensued.

His strange behavior began to render me uneasy. It is well to know something of a person confined with you in a small room at the dead of night, and I was about to address the fellow when he began stealthily approaching the bed. He might have been three yards distant when I arose to a sitting posture. This caused him to pause, his form well within the streak of light. Resting upon the edge of the bed and facing him, my own features were clearly disclosed, and we examined each other curiously.

I had never seen him before, and I had little pleasure in meeting him then. He appeared to be a man at least fifty years of age, with pallid, sunken cheeks, eyes bright, but shifting in their gaze, and scanty gray locks that now hung disordered over a low forehead. His form was thin and angular, his clothing of mean quality, and his hands, which dangled before him at the ends of the short chain, were large and hardened by toil.

Not a Brazilian, I decided at once; but I could not then determine his probable nationality.

"Likewise a prisoner, señor?" he inquired, in an indistinct, mumbling tone, and with a strong accent.

"Yes," I answered.

"Ah, conspirator. I see; I see!" He nodded his head several times, and then growled sentences that I could not understand.

While I stared at him he turned away again, and with a soft and stealthy tread made the entire circuit of the room, feeling of each piece of furniture it contained, and often pausing for many moments in one spot as if occupied in deep thought.

At last he approached the bed again, dragging after him a chair in which he slowly seated himself opposite me.

"Retain your couch, señor," he muttered. "I shall not disturb you, and it will soon be morning. You may sleep."

But I was now fully awake, and had no intention of sleeping while this strange individual occupied his seat beside me.

"Who are you?" I demanded. "A patriot?"

"Not as you use the term," he answered, at once. "I am Mexican."

"Mexican!" I echoed, surprised. "Do you speak English?"

"Truly, señor," he answered, but his English was as bad as his Portuguese.

"Why are you here and a prisoner?" I asked.

"I had business with Señor de Pintra. I came from afar to see him, but found the soldiers inhabiting his house. I am timid, señor, and suspecting trouble I hid in an out-building, where the soldiers discovered me. Why I should be arrested I do not know. I am not conspirator; I am not even Brazilian. I do not care for your politics whatever. They tell me Miguel de Pintra is dead. Is it true?"

His tone did not seem sincere. But I replied it was true that Dom Miguel was dead.

"Then I should be allowed to depart. But not so. They tell me the great Emperor is here, their Dom Pedro, and he will speak to me in the morning. Is it true?"

This time I detected an anxiety in his voice that told me he had not suspected the Emperor's presence until his arrest.

But I answered that Dom Pedro was then occupying de Pintra's mansion, together with many of his important ministers.

For a time he remained silent, probably considering the matter with care. But he was ill at ease, and shifted continually in his chair.

"You are Americano?" he asked at last.

"Yes," said I.

"I knew, when you ask me for my English. But why does the Emperor arrest an American?"

I smiled; but there was no object in trying to deceive him.

"I was private secretary to Dom Miguel," said I, "and they suspect my late master to have plotted against the Emperor."

He laughed, unpleasantly.

"It is well your master is dead when they make that suspicion," said he; then paused a moment and asked, abruptly, "Did he tell you of the vault?"

I stared at him. A Mexican, not a conspirator, yet aware of the secret vault! It occurred to me that it would be well to keep my own counsel, for a time, at least.

"A vault?" I asked, carelessly, and shook my head.

Again the fellow laughed disagreeably. But my answer seemed to have pleased him.

"He was sly! Ah, he was sly, the dear Señor Miguel!" he chuckled, rocking his thin form back and forth upon the chair. "But never mind. It is nothing. I never pry into secrets, señor. It is not my nature."

I said nothing and another silent fit seized him. Perhaps five minutes had passed before he arose and made a second stealthy circuit of the room, this time examining the barred window with great care. Then he sighed heavily and came back to his seat.

"What will be your fate, señor?" he asked.

"I shall appeal to our consul at Rio. They must release me," I answered.

"Good. Very good! They must release you. You are no conspirator—a mere secretary, and an American."

I nodded, wishing I might share his confidence. Presently he asked for my name and residence, and I answered him truly.

"I myself am Manuel Pesta, of the City of Mexico. You must not forget the name, señor. Manuel Pesta, the clockmaker."

"I shall not forget," said I, wondering what he could mean. And a moment later he startled me by bending forward and asking in an eager tone:

"Have they searched you?"

"Yes."

"It is my turn soon. This morning."

He leaned back in his chair, closed his eyes, and fell silent again.

For my part I lay back upon the pillow, yet taking care to face him, and so we remained until daylight came and gradually drove the shadows from the little room.

Even then my strange companion did not move. He was indeed a queer mixture of eager activity and absolute self-repression. Another hour passed, and then we heard footsteps approaching down the passageway.

With a start Pesta aroused himself and fixed a searching glance upon my face. Trembling with nervousness he suddenly raised his manacled hands and removed from his mouth a small object that glittered in the morning light.

My heart gave a sudden bound. *It was the ring that opened the secret vault!*

His own agitation prevented his noting my amazement. Thrusting the ring toward me he whispered, hurriedly:

"Conceal it, quickly, for the love of God! Keep it until I come for it—I, Manuel Pesta—until I demand it of Robert Harcliffe of New Orleans. It may be today—it may be many days. But I will come, señor, I—"

The bolts of the door shot back and a squad of soldiers entered. Their sudden appearance barely gave me time to drop the ring into an outside pocket of my coat. As two of the soldiers seized him I noticed that the Mexican was trembling violently; but he arose meekly and submitted to be led from the room. Two others motioned me to follow, and in a few moments we were ushered into the room where I had had my interview with the Emperor.

Valcour was standing by the fireplace when we entered, and eyeing the Mexican with indifference he said to the captain:

"This is the man you found secreted in the out-building?"

"It is, senhor," answered the captain.

"Have you searched him?"

"Only partially. We took from him this revolver, a knife, and this purse. There were no papers."

Valcour took the weapons in his hands and examined them. The revolver, I could see as he threw back the barrel, was loaded in all six chambers. The knife he glanced at and turned to place upon the mantel when a second thought seemingly induced him to open the blades. It was a large, two-bladed affair, and the bright steel showed that it was sharpened as finely as a razor. As I watched the Emperor's spy I chanced to look toward the Mexican and surprised an expression that nearly resembled terror upon his haggard face. Perhaps Valcour saw it, too, for he drew a handkerchief from his pocket and carefully wiped out the seats in the handles where the blades lay when the knife was closed. A small stain appeared upon the linen, and the spy carried the handkerchief to the window and inspected the stain with interest. While he was thus engaged the Emperor entered the room, followed by his ministers, and seating himself at the table calmly proceeded to light a cigar. Evidently he had just breakfasted, for he had an appearance of content that indicated a comfortable condition.

Valcour, returning from the window, first saluted the Emperor with great deference, and then addressed the Mexican.

"Why did you kill that man last evening and sever his hand with your knife?"

The Mexican gazed at him in horror.

"I—señor, as God hears me, I—"

"Tell me why!" said Valcour calmly.

The fellow glared at him as if fascinated. Then he threw his hands, all manacled as they were, high above his head, and with a scream that caused even the Emperor to start, fell upon the floor in a swoon.

Valcour turned him over with his foot.

"Search him!" he commanded.

The men were thorough. Not a shred of clothing escaped their eyes. And after they had finished the detective himself made an examination.

Dom Pedro was evidently much interested. Without any explanation further than Valcour's accusation, all present understood that the Mexican was charged with the murder of the man found in the shrubbery and therefore he must either have the ring upon his person or had deposited it in some secret place.

He lay unconscious after the search had ended, and Valcour, after a moment's reflection, ordered the men to carry him back to the room where he had passed the night, to guard him well, and to send for a physician.

The Emperor relighted his cigar, which had gone out, and in the interval I heard the sound of a troupe of horse galloping up the drive. There was no mistaking the clank of sabers, and Dom Pedro leaned forward with an expectant look upon his face, in which the others joined.

Then the door burst open and a man entered and knelt before the Emperor. I could scarcely restrain a cry of surprise as I saw him.

It was Francisco Paola.

XV

A Dangerous Moment

Not since I parted with him in the road on the morning of Dom Miguel's murder had I seen Paola or heard from him directly.

At that time, after giving me two men who had proved faithful both to me and the Cause, he had ridden on to the house of death—"to breakfast with his sister." From that moment his actions had been a mystery not only to me but to all his fellow-conspirators.

But now it seemed easy to understand that the Minister of Police had been attending to the Emperor's business, and that he had also been playing a double game from the beginning, and promoting the revolution that he might the more easily crush it.

As he rose to his feet after saluting the Emperor, Paola glanced around the room and noted my presence. I could not well disguise the scorn I felt for this treacherous fellow, and as he met my eyes he smiled and twirled his small moustache with a satisfied air.

"Well?" demanded the Emperor.

"All is indeed well, your Majesty," returned the minister, lightly. "The leaders of the conspiracy, with one exception, are now under arrest."

"And that one?"

"Sanchez Bastro, a coffee-planter with a ranch near by. He has crossed the border. But it is unimportant."

"And Mendez?"

"Imprisoned in the citadel."

"Barros?"

"He is comforting Mendez, in the same cell."

"Treverot?"

"Unfortunately we were obliged to shoot him. He chose to resist."

"Hm! And Piexoto?"

"Is below, under arrest."

"Have him brought here." The captain left the room, and again the Emperor turned to Paola.

"You have done well, senhor; and your reward shall be adequate. It was a far-reaching plot, and dangerous." And Dom Pedro sighed as if greatly relieved.

Paola brushed a speck of dust from his sleeve and laughed in his silly fashion.

"The serpent is only dangerous, your Majesty, until its fangs are pulled," he drawled, and strolled away toward Valcour, while the soldiers brought in Senhor Floriano Piexoto.

The famous patriot was not only hand-cuffed, but his elbows were bound together by cords across his back. But despite his bonds he walked proudly and scowled into Dom Pedro's face as he confronted him. Indeed, I was filled with admiration to find that this man whom Fonseca had called "croaker" could be brave when occasion demanded it.

"So, my clever statesman has seen fit to turn traitor," began the Emperor, sternly regarding the prisoner.

"A champion of Liberty must needs be a traitor to Dom Pedro," replied Piexoto, with equal sternness.

"But the conspiracy is at an end, and I am inclined to be merciful," resumed the Emperor. "I am told you were the trusted friend of Miguel de Pintra, and knew his secrets. If you will inform us how to unlock the secret vault, I will promise to regard your offense lightly."

Piexoto stared at him a moment indignantly. Then he turned with a frown upon Paola.

"Ask of your Minister of Police," he retorted; "for there stands a double traitor! It was he who stood closest to de Pintra, winning his confidence only to betray it. It was Francisco Paola who planned the secret vault. Who should know better than he how to open it?"

The Emperor turned to Paola with suspicion written visibly upon his stern features.

"Did you plan the vault?" he demanded.

"Truly, your Majesty. Otherwise the records would have been scattered in many places. I planned the vault that all might be concentrated in one place—where we should find them when we were ready to explode the conspiracy. Records—plans—money—all are now at our hand."

"But we have not the key. Why did you plan so complicated a lock?"

"Nothing else would have satisfied de Pintra. As for the lock, it is nothing. A drill through one of the steel panels would have admitted us easily. But—"

"But what, sir? Why do we not drill now, instead of seeking this cursed ring?"

The Minister smiled and again twirled his moustaches.

"Because Dom Miguel suddenly developed inventive genius on his own part. I was absent when the work was completed, and too late I discovered that de Pintra had made pockets everywhere between the steel plates, and filled every pocket with nitro-glycerine."

"Well?"

"That is all. To drill into the vault is to explode a pocket of nitro-glycerine, which in turn will explode all the other pockets through concussion."

"And then?"

"And then the contents of the vault would be blown to atoms. Of the mansion itself not one stone would remain upon another. The records we seek would be lost irrevocably."

Valcour, pale with fear, uttered a cry and dashed through the door, while the Emperor rose to his feet with a look of terror upon his face.

"They are drilling now!" he gasped.

Silently we stood, none daring to move; and into our drawn faces Piexoto gazed with a grim and derisive smile.

Paolo, more composed than any of the others, except Piexoto, began rolling a cigarette, but remembering the Emperor's presence he ceased.

And so we stood, motionless and silent, until footsteps were again heard and Valcour re-entered wiping the perspiration from his forehead with an embroidered handkerchief. His face wore a look of relief, but there was a slight tremor in his voice as he said:

"I have ordered the drilling stopped, your Majesty."

Dom Pedro, thus reassured, strode back and forth in evident perplexity.

"We must have the key!" he said, angrily. "There is no other way. And the key cannot be far off. Has your prisoner, the Mexican, recovered?"

"I will go and see," answered the detective, and again left the room.

I caught a look of surprise upon the face of the Minister of Police. It was fleeting, but I was sure it had been there.

"May I inquire who this prisoner is?" he asked. One of the men who acted as secretary to the Emperor, receiving a nod from Dom Pedro, informed Paola of the finding of the dead body in the shrubbery, and of the consequent arrest of the Mexican.

"And the key was not found in his possession?" he inquired, eagerly.

"No."

"Then he secreted it, fearing arrest. Have the out-buildings been searched?"

"Not yet."

"Let it be done at once."

Valcour, entering in time to hear this, flushed angrily.

"That is my business, Senhor Paola. I will brook no interference from the police."

"Ah! had it not been for the police, Senhor Valcour would have blown his Emperor into eternity," returned Paola, smiling blandly into the spy's disturbed countenance.

"Enough of this!" cried the Emperor. "Let the grounds and outbuildings be carefully searched. Is your prisoner recovered, Valcour?"

"He is raving mad," returned the detective, in a surly tone. "It requires two soldiers to control him."

I breathed a sigh of relief, for I had feared the Mexican, in his terror, would betray the fact that he had given me the ring.

XVI

Traitor to the Cause

The Emperor retired while the search of the grounds was being conducted, and Piexoto and I were escorted to another room upon the ground floor and locked in. There were two unbarred windows looking upon the grounds, but a sentry was posted at each of these, and as we were still hand-cuffed, our escape was impossible.

For a time my companion did nothing but curse Paola in the most hearty and diversified manner, and I made no effort to stop him. But finally this amusement grew monotonous even to its author, and he asked me how I had allowed myself to be captured.

I therefore related my adventures, but said nothing about the ring.

"I have always suspected Paola," he told me, "and often warned Dom Miguel against him. The man's very nature is frivolous. He could not be expected to keep faith. Yet it is surprising he did not choose to betray the Emperor, rather than us; for the Revolution is too powerful and too far advanced to be quelled by the arrest of a few of its leaders."

"But what of Fonseca?" I asked curiously. "Why was he not arrested also? Why was not his name mentioned to the Emperor?"

"I confess the fact puzzles me," returned Piexoto, thoughtfully. "Fonseca is even more compromised than I am myself, and unless he had a secret understanding with Paola, and purchased immunity, I cannot account for his escaping arrest."

"But the general will not forsake the cause, I am sure," I said, earnestly. "And it seems that Senhor Bastro, also, has succeeded in eluding arrest. Therefore, should the royalists fail to find the key to the vault, all may yet be well, in spite of Paola's treachery."

"There is another perplexing matter," returned Piexoto, pacing the room in deep thought. "Miguel de Pintra never told me the vault was sheathed with nitro-glycerine. Did you know it?"

"Yes," I answered. "But the secret was revealed to me by Lesba Paola, the Minister's sister."

"I can scarcely believe it, nevertheless," he resumed. "Yet what object could the traitor have in preventing their reaching the records, unless he knew the attempt to drill through the walls would destroy us all—himself included?"

"Perhaps he has fear that the records would incriminate him with the Emperor," I suggested.

"Bah! He has made his terms, evidently. That he worked faithfully in our interests for a time is quite believable; but either the Emperor's bribes were too tempting or he lost faith in the Cause."

I was about to reply when the door opened to admit Paola. Piexoto paused in his walk to glare at the Minister, and I was myself no less surprised at the inopportune visit.

But Paola, with the old, smirking smile upon his face that nothing ever seemed to banish, nodded pleasantly at us and sat down in an easy-chair. He rolled a cigarette and carefully lighted it before he addressed us.

"Senhors, you are about to denounce me as a traitor to the Cause," said he; "but you may both spare your words. Before the Cause existed I was Minister to the Emperor. A policeman walks in devious paths. If I am true to the oath I gave the Emperor, how dare you, Floriano Piexoto, who have violated yours, condemn me?"

"I don't," answered the other. "It is absurd to condemn a man like you. Treachery is written on every line of your false face. My only regret is that I did not kill you long ago."

"Yet the chief, Dom Miguel de Pintra, trusted me," remarked Paola, in a musing tone, at the same time flicking the ash from his cigarette with a deliberate gesture. "He was, it seems, the only one."

"Not so," said I, angry at his insolent bearing. "Your sister, sir, had faith in you."

He looked at me with a quizzical expression, and laughed. I had ventured the remark in an endeavor to pierce his shield of conceit and indifference. But it seemed that even Lesba's misplaced confidence failed to shame him, for at that moment the girl's loyalty to the Cause seemed to me beyond a doubt.

"My sister was, I believe, an ardent republican. Poor little girl! How could she judge the merits of a political controversy? But there, senhors, let us have done with chidings. I am come for the key."

Piexoto and I stared at each other aghast. The key! Could the Minister suspect either of us of possessing it?

"Quite prettily acted, gentlemen," he resumed, "but it is useless to oppose my request. I suppose our friend Harcliffe has passed it on to you, senhor? No? Then he must have it on his person."

"Are you mad?" I asked, with well-assumed contempt.

"No; but the Mexican is. I have just left his room, and he raves perpetually of a ring he has given to Robert Harcliffe, of New Orleans. A ring that must be restored to him on demand."

"He raves," said I, coolly, although my heart was beating wildly.

"He does, indeed," acknowledged Paola. "And he tells exactly where the ring was placed—in the outer pocket of your jacket. Will you pardon me, senhor, if I prove the truth of his assertion?"

He rose and advanced to me with a soft, stealthy tread, and I backed away until I stood fairly against the wall, vainly endeavoring to find some way to circumvent him.

"Hold!" cried a clear voice, and as Paola swung around upon his heel I saw beyond him the form of Valcour outlined by the dark doorway.

"You were doubtless about to search the prisoner, senhor," said the spy, calmly, as he approached us. "I have myself just come from the Mexican's room and heard his ravings. But the task must be mine, since the Emperor has placed the search for the key in my hands."

Paola turned with a slight shrug and resumed his seat.

"I have searched the prisoner already," he announced, "but failed to find the ring. Doubtless he has passed it to Piexoto, or secreted it. Or, it may be, the Mexican's words are mere ravings."

The detective hesitated.

"Who is this Mexican, Senhor Paola?" he asked.

"Frankly, I do not know. Not a conspirator, I am sure, and evidently not a royalist."

"Then how came he to know of the existence of the ring?"

"A mystery, my dear Valcour. Have you yet identified the man this Mexican murdered?"

"Not yet."

"I myself have not had a good look at the body. If you will take me to him I will endeavor to locate the fellow. It was doubtless he who murdered Madam Izabel."

As he spoke he rose and walked quietly toward the door, as if he expected Valcour to follow. But the spy, suddenly suspicious, cast a shrewd glance at me and replied:

"One moment, Senhor Paola. I must satisfy myself that neither Harcliffe nor Piexoto has the ring, in order that I may report to the Emperor."

"As you like," returned the Minister, indifferently, and resumed his chair.

Valcour came straight to my side, thrust his hand within my pocket, and drew out the ring.

"Ah!" he cried, his face lighting with joy, "your search must have been a careless one, my dear Paola! Here is news for the Emperor, at last."

He hurried from the room, and Paola, still smiling, rose and faced us.

"It is a great pity," said he, pleasantly, with his eyes on my face, "that God permits any man to be a fool."

Before I could reply he had followed Valcour from the room, and Piexoto, regarding me with a sullen frown, exclaimed:

"I can say amen to that! Why did you not tell me you had the ring?"

I did not reply. The taunts and the loss of the ring had dazed me and I sank into a chair and covered my eyes with my hands.

Pacing the room with furious energy, Piexoto growled a string of laments and reproaches into my unwilling ears.

"My poor comrades! It is their death-warrant. These records will condemn to punishment half the great families of Brazil. And now when the battle is almost won, to have them fall into the Emperor's hands. Thank God, de Pintra is dead! This blow would be worse to him than death itself."

"However," said I, somewhat recovering myself, "we shall now secure his body from that grim vault. That is one satisfaction, at least."

He did not see fit to reply to this, but paced the floor in as great agitation as before.

Captain de Souza entered with two of his guards.

"The Emperor commands you to unlock the vault," he said to me. "Be good enough to follow, senhor. And Senhor Piexoto is also requested to be present."

"Tell the Emperor I refuse to unlock the vault," I returned, firmly.

"And why?" demanded Piexoto, scornfully. "It is merely a question of time, now that they have the key, when they will find the right indentation in the door."

"True," I answered. Then, to the captain: "Lead on, I will follow."

They escorted us to the library and down the winding stair until we stood in the well-known chamber at the end of the passage. The outer door of the vault lay open, displaying the steel surface of the inner door, with its countless indentations.

The Emperor and his secretary, together with Paola and Valcour, were awaiting us. The latter handed me the ring.

"His Majesty commands you to open the door, senhor Americano," he said.

"I believe the Minister of Police designed this vault. Let him open it himself," I replied, my resolution halting at the thought of what the open door would reveal.

"Yes, I designed it," said the Minister, "but I did not execute the work. Doubtless in time I could open the door; but the Emperor is impatient."

I saw that further resistance was useless. Bending over, I fitted the stone of the ring into the proper indentation, and shot the bolts. The great door was swung upward, a whiff of the damp, confined air entered my nostrils and made me shiver.

Reaching my hand within the vault I turned the switch that threw on the electric light, and then withdrew that the others might enter.

But no one moved. The light illuminated the full interior of the great vault, and every eye gazed eagerly within.

Valcour uttered a groan of baffled rage; Piexoto swore horribly in a scarcely audible tone, and the Minister of Police laughed.

"Good God!" cried the Emperor, with staring eyeballs, *the vault is empty!*"

XVII

The Torch of Rebellion

With a bound I stood within the grim vault and searched its confines with anxious eyes. True enough, the place was empty. Not a scrap of paper, a book, or a bank-note had been left there. The shelves that lined the walls were as bare as Mother Hubbard's cupboard.

The records of the Revolution were gone. The body of Miguel de Pintra was gone. Thank God, the great and glorious Cause was as yet safe!

Valcour was on his hands and knees, prying into the corners for some scrap that might have been overlooked.

Paola stood beside me with the old aggravating simper upon his face, twirling one end of his moustache.

Suddenly Valcour stood up and faced him.

"Traitor!" he cried, with a passionate gesture, "it is you who have done this! It is you who have led us here only to humiliate us and laugh at us!"

"Your Majesty," said Paola, without moving his head, "will you kindly protect me from the insults of your servants?"

"Have peace, Valcour!" growled the Emperor. "Senhor Francisco has proved his loyalty, and doubtless shares our chagrin. Come, gentlemen, let us leave this dismal place."

I followed slowly in the train of the party as it wound its way through the narrow passage and up the iron stairs into the library. My hand-cuffs had been removed when I was brought to open the vault, and an idea came to me to lag behind and try to effect my escape from the house.

But Valcour was waiting for me at the trap door, and called Captain de Souza to guard me. I was taken to the large room on the ground floor, from whence they had brought me, thrust through the doorway, and the key turned upon me.

Piexoto had been taken elsewhere, and I found myself alone.

My thoughts were naturally confused by the amazing discovery we had just made, and I was so engaged in wondering what had become of Dom Miguel and the records that I scarcely looked up when the door opened to admit Francisco Paola.

He had in his hand a small parcel that looked like a box, which he placed upon a table near the open window.

Next he drew a note-book from his pocket, scribbled some lines upon three several leaves, and then, tearing them out, he reached within the box, taking care to lift but a portion of the cover, and busied himself some moments in a way that made me wonder what he could be doing. I had no suspicion of the truth until he carried the box to the window and quickly removed the cover. Then, although his back was toward me, I heard a rapid flutter of wings, followed by a strange silence, and I knew that Paola was following with his eyes the flight of the birds he had liberated.

"So, my dear Minister, I have at last discovered your secret!" said a sharp voice, and as Paola whirled about I noted that Valcour had entered the room and was standing with folded arms and eyes that sparkled triumphantly.

"Orders to my men," remarked the Minister, quietly, and brushed a small feather from his arm.

"True enough!" retorted Valcour, with a bitter smile. "Orders to General Fonseca, whom you strangely overlooked in making your decoy arrests. Orders to Sanchez Bastro, who is to distribute arms to the rebels! And where did the third pigeon go, my loyal and conscientious Minister of Police? To Mazanovitch, or to that Miguel de Pintra whom you falsely led us to believe had perished in yonder vault?"

He came close to the Minister.

"Traitor! In setting free these birds you have fired the torch of rebellion; that terrible flame which is liable to sweep the land, and consume royalist and republican alike!"

Paola, the sneering smile for once gone from his face, gazed at his accuser with evident admiration.

"You are wonderfully clever, my dear Valcour," said he, slowly. "You have wit; you have a clear judgment; your equal is not in all Brazil. What a pity, my friend, that you are not one of us!"

Somehow, the words seemed to ring true.

Valcour flushed to the roots of his hair.

"I hate you," he cried, stamping his foot with passion. "You have thwarted me always. You have laughed at me—sneered at me—defied me! But at last I have you in the toils. Francisco Paola, I arrest you in the name of the Emperor."

"On what charge?"

"The charge of treason!"

Paola laughed softly, and in a tone denoting genuine amusement.

"Come, my brave detective," said he; "we will go to the Emperor together, and accuse each other to our hearts' content!"

He attempted to take Valcour's arm, in his inimitable jaunty fashion; but the spy shook him off and followed Paola from the room, trembling with suppressed rage.

For my part, I knew not what to make of the scene, except that these men were bitter enemies, and each endeavoring to destroy the other. But could Valcour's accusation be true? Had the torch of revolution really been fired?

God forbid that I should ever meet with such another man as Francisco Paola again! Deep or shallow, coxcomb or clever conspirator, true man or traitor—it was as impossible to read him or to judge his real character as to solve the mighty, unfathomable secrets of Nature.

One moment I called him traitor; the next I was sure he was faithful to the Cause. But who could judge the man aright? Not I, indeed!

Thus reflecting, I approached the window and looked out. Eight feet below me one of the Uruguayan guards paced back and forth upon the green lawn, his short carbine underneath his arm, and a poniard swinging at his side.

The fellow looked up and saw me.

"Close that window!" he commanded, with a scowl.

I obeyed, sliding the sash to its place. But still I gazed through the glass at the labyrinth of walks and hedges defining the extensive gardens at this side of the house. I knew every inch of these grounds, having wandered there many hours during my sojourn at the mansion. And the thought came to me that it would not be difficult to escape in that maze of hedge and shrubbery, had I once a fair start of my pursuers.

Within my range of vision was a portion of the driveway, and presently I saw the Emperor's carriage roll away, followed by several others. Piexoto was seated in the last of the carriages, but only a small portion of the Uruguayan guard accompanied the cortège.

I tried to see if the Minister of Police was among those who were returning to Rio, but was unable to note his presence in the brief time the carriages were in view. Nor did Valcour seem to be with them. Captain de Souza evidently remained in charge of the guards left at the mansion.

Well, I longed to leave the place myself, now that the emptiness of the secret vault had been disclosed; but for some reason my captors desired me to remain a prisoner.

The day dragged wearily away. One of the Uruguayans brought me food at noontime, and I ate with good appetite. The room grew close, but when I attempted to raise the window the surly guard outside presented his carbine, and I respected his wish to leave the sash lowered.

During this time I had ample opportunity to speculate upon the astonishing events of the morning; but my attempt to solve the problem of what had become of Dom Miguel and the records seemed absolutely futile. That the body of the chief had been removed by some friendly hand—the same that had saved the funds and papers—there was no doubt whatever. But when had this removal taken place?

At one time a fleeting hope animated me that the vault had been entered in time to save Dom Miguel from suffocation; but a little reflection soon caused me to abandon that notion. Allowing that the slayer of Madam Izabel had been a patriot, and left the train at the first station beyond Cruz, he could not possibly have returned to de Pintra's mansion on the swiftest horse within eight hours of the time my friend had been entombed alive, and long before that Dom Miguel would have succumbed to the confined atmosphere of his prison.

Moreover, none of the conspirators who knew of the ring or was competent to recognize it had been on the train at the time of Izabel de Mar's death. Therefore the patriot who finally secured the key to the vault and saved the records must have obtained the ring long after any hope of saving the life of the imprisoned chief had been abandoned.

Somehow, it occurred to me that the man in the shrubbery had not been murdered by the Mexican, but by someone of our band who had promptly cleared the vault and escaped with the contents—even while the Emperor and his party were in possession of the house. The ring might have been dropped during the escape and found by the Mexican—this being the only plausible way to account for its being in his possession.

Although these speculations were to some extent a diversion, and served to occupy my thoughts during my tedious confinement, there were many details to contradict their probability, and I was not at all positive that I had discovered the right explanation of the mystery.

It must have been near evening when the door was again opened. This time a man was thrust into the room and the door quickly locked upon us.

I started from my chair with an exclamation of dismay. My fellow-prisoner was the mad Mexican!

XVIII

A Narrow Escape

The man did not seem to notice my presence at first. For a time he remained motionless in the position the guards had left him, his vacant eyes fixed steadily upon the opposite wall.

Then, with a long-drawn sigh, his gaze fell and wandered to the table where stood the remains of my luncheon. With a wolflike avidity he pounced upon the tray, eagerly consuming every scrap that I had left, and draining a small bottle of wine of the last dregs it contained.

When he had finished he still continued to fumble about the tray, and presently picked up a large, two-tined steel fork and examined it with careful attention. They had brought no knife into the room, and I had scarcely noticed the fork before; yet now, as the Mexican held it firmly in his clinched fist, and passed it to and fro with a serpent-like motion, I realized with a thrill of anxiety that it might prove a terrible weapon in the hands of a desperate man.

Evidently my fellow-prisoner had the same thought, for after a time he concealed the fork in his bosom, and then turned to examine the room more carefully. His first act was to approach the window, and when he started and shrank away I knew our ever-vigilant guard had warned him not to consider that avenue of escape.

Next he swung around and faced the place where I sat, slightly in the shadow. The day was drawing to its close, and he had not noticed me before. A swift motion toward his breast was followed by a smile, and he advanced close to me and said, in his stumbling English:

"Aha! My American frien' to which I gave the ring! It is safe, señor? It is safe?"

I nodded, thinking to humor him. Indeed, I could not determine at that moment whether the man was still insane or not.

He drew a chair to my side and sat down.

"Listen, then, my frien'. Together we will find riches—riches very great! Why? Because we Mexicans—Careno and myself—we build the door of the big vault under this house. So? They bring us here blindfold. We work many days on the big plate with strange device cut in the steel. Careno was expert. Only one place, cut with great cunning, shot the bolts in their sockets. For myself, I am clockmaker and gem-cutter. They tell me to cut emerald so it fit the plate, and mount it in ring. Yes, it was I, Señor Americano, who do that fine work—I, Manuel Pesta!

"Then they carry us away, blindfold again, to the border of Uruguay. We do not know this house—we cannot find it again ever. So they think. But to make sure they hire men to assassinate us—to stab us to the heart in those Uruguay Mountain. Fine pay for our work—eh, señor? But, peste! Careno and I—we stab our assassins—we escape—we swear vengeance! For two year we wander in Brazil—seeking, ever seeking for the house with the vault.

"How clever they are! But we, are we not also clever? On a railway train one day we see a lady with the ring! We cannot mistake—I made it, and I know my work. It is key to the big vault! Careno cannot wait. He sit beside lady and put his knife in her heart. The train rattle along and the lady make no noise. But the ring sticks, so Careno cuts off finger and puts in pocket. Are we not clever, señor? Now we have ring, but yet know not of the house with the vault. We keep quiet and ride on to Rio. There the dead lady is carried out and all is excitement. She is Señora Izabel de Mar, daughter of Dom Miguel de Pintra. She come from her father's house at Cuyaba. This we hear and remember. Then a man they call Valcour he rush up and cry, 'Her finger is gone! The ring—where is the ring?' Aha! we know now we are right.

"So we go away and find out about Miguel de Pintra—the head of great rebellion with millions of gold and notes to pay the soldiers when they fight. Good! We know now of the vault. We know we have key. We know we are now rich! Careno and I we go to Cuyaba—we find this house—we hide in the bushes till night. Then Careno get mad for the money—he want it all, not half—and he try to murder me. Ah, well! my pistol is quicker than his knife, that is all. He is wearing ring, and it stick like it stick on lady's hand. Bah! I cut off Careno's hand and carve away the ring. It is simple, is it not?

"But now the soldiers gallop up. The house is fill with people. So I must wait. I hide in secret place, but soon they drag me out and make me prisoner. What! must I lose all now—millions—millions of gold—and no Careno to share it? No! I am still clever. I keep ring in mouth until I meet you, and I give it to you to keep. When they search me, there is no ring."

He sprang up, chuckling and rubbing his hands together in great delight. He danced a step or two and then drew the steel fork from his breast and struck it fiercely into the table-top, standing silently to watch it while the prongs quivered and came to rest.

"Am I not clever?" he again asked, drawing out the fork from the wood and returning it to his breast. "But I am generous, too. You shall divide with me. But not half! I won all from Careno, but you shall have some—enough to be rich, Señor Americano. And now, give me the ring!"

By this time his eyes were glittering with insanity, and at his abrupt demand I shifted uneasily in my seat, not knowing how to reply.

"Give me the ring!" he repeated, a tone of menace creeping into his high-pitched voice.

I arose and walked toward the window, getting the table between us. Then I turned and faced him.

"They have taken the ring from me," I said.

He stood as if turned to stone, his fierce eyes fixed upon my own.

"They have opened the vault with it," I continued, "and found it bare and empty."

He gave a shrill scream at this, and began trembling in every limb.

"You lie!" he shouted, wildly. "You try to cheat me—to get all! And the vault has millions—millions in gold and notes. Give me the ring!"

I made no reply. To reiterate my assertion would do no good, and the man was incompetent to consider the matter calmly. Indeed, he once more drew that ugly fork from his breast and, grasping it as one would a dagger, began creeping toward me with a stealthy, cat-like tread.

I approached the edge of the round center-table, alert to keep its breadth between me and my companion. The Mexican paused opposite me, and whispered between his clinched teeth:

"Give it me! Give me the ring!"

"The guard will be here presently," said I, fervently hoping I spoke the truth, "and he will tell you of the ring. I am quite sure Senhor Valcour has it."

"Ah, I am betrayed! You wish to take all—you and this Valcour! But see, my Americano—I will kill you. I will kill you now, and then you have nothing for your treachery!"

Slowly he edged his way around the table, menacing me with his strange weapon, and with my eyes fixed upon his I moved in the opposite direction, retaining the table as my shield.

First in one direction and then in the other he moved, swiftly at times, then with deliberate caution, striving ever to take me unawares and reach me with his improvised dagger.

This situation could not stand the tension for long; I realized that sooner or later the game must have an abrupt ending.

So, as I dodged my persistent enemy, I set my wits working to devise a means of escape. The window seemed my only hope, and I had lost all fear of the sentry in the more terrible danger that confronted me.

Suddenly I exerted my strength and thrust the table against the Mexican so forcibly that he staggered backward. Then I caught up a chair and after a swing around my head hurled it toward him like a catapult. It crushed him to the floor, and e'er he could rise again I had thrown up the sash of the window and leaped out.

Fortune often favors the desperate. I alighted full upon the form of the unsuspecting sentry, bearing him to the ground by my weight, where we both rolled in the grass.

Quickly I regained my feet and darted away into the flower-garden, seeking to reach the hedges before my guard could recover himself.

Over my shoulder I saw him kneeling and deliberately pointing at me his carbine. Before he could fire the flying form of the Mexican descended upon him from the window. There was a flash and a report, but the ball went wide its mark, and instantly the two men were struggling in a death-grapple upon the lawn.

Away I ran through the maze of hedge and shrubbery, threading the well-known paths unerringly. I heard excited shouts as the guardsmen, aroused by their comrade's shot, poured from the mansion and plunged into the gardens to follow me. But it was dusk by this time, and I had little fear of being overtaken.

The estate was bounded upon this side by an impenetrable thick-set hedge, but it was broken in one place by a gardeners' tool-house, which had a door at each side, and thus admitted one into a lane that wound through a grove and joined the main highway a mile beyond.

Reaching this tool-house I dashed within, closed and barred the door behind me, and then emerged upon the lane.

To my surprise I saw a covered carriage standing in the gloom, and made out that the door stood open and a man upon the box was holding the reins and leaning toward me eagerly as if striving to solve my identity.

Without hesitation I sprang into the carriage and closed the door, crying to the man:

"Quick! for your life—drive on!"

Without a word he lashed his horses and we started with a jerk that threw me into the back seat.

I heard an exclamation in a woman's startled voice and felt a muffled form shrinking into the corner of the carriage. Then two shots rang out; I heard a scream and the sound of a fall as the driver pitched upon the ground, and now like the wind the maddened horses rushed on without guidance, swaying the carriage from side to side with a dangerous motion.

These Brazilian carriages have a trap in the top to permit the occupants to speak to the driver. I found this trap, threw it upward, and drew myself up until I was able to scramble into the vacant seat. The reins had fallen between the horses, evidently, but we were now dashing through the grove, and the shadows were so deep that I could distinguish nothing distinctly.

Cautiously I let myself down until my feet touched the pole, and then, resting my hands upon the loins of the madly galloping animals, I succeeded in grasping the reins and returned safely to the box seat.

Then I braced myself to conquer the runaways, and when we emerged from the grove and came upon the highway there was sufficient light for me to keep the horses in the straight road until they had tired themselves sufficiently to be brought under control.

During this time I had turned to speak a reassuring word, now and then, to the unknown woman in the carriage.

Doubtless she had been both amazed and indignant at my abrupt seizure of her equipage; but there was not yet time to explain to her my necessity.

We were headed straight for the station at Cuyaba, and I decided at once to send a telegram warning Mazanovitch of danger. For Paola had turned traitor, the vault had been opened, and the Emperor was even now on his way to Rio to arrest all who had previously escaped the net of the Minister of Police.

So we presently dashed up to the station, which was nearly deserted at this hour, and after calling a porter to hold the horses I went into the station to write my telegram.

Mazanovitch had asked me to use but one word, and although I had much of interest to communicate, a moment's thought assured me that a warning of danger was sufficient.

So, after a brief hesitation, I wrote the word "Lesba," and handed the message to the operator.

"That is my name, senhor," said a soft voice behind me, and I turned to confront Lesba Paola.

XIX

The Wayside Inn

Astonishment rendered me speechless, and at first I could do no more than bow with an embarrassed air to the cloaked figure before me. Lesba's fair face, peering from beneath her mantilla, was grave but set, and her brilliant eyes bore a questioning and half-contemptuous look that was hard to meet.

"That is my name, senhor," she repeated, "and you will oblige me by explaining why you are sending it to Captain Mazanovitch."

"Was it your carriage in which I escaped?" I inquired.

"Yes; and my man now lies wounded by the roadside. Why did you take me by surprise, Senhor Harcliffe? And why—*why* are you telegraphing my name to Mazanovitch?"

Although my thoughts were somewhat confused I remembered that Lesba had accompanied her brother to Rio; that her brother had turned traitor, and she herself had ridden in the Emperor's carriage, with the spy Valcour. And I wondered how it was that her carriage should have been standing this very evening at a retired spot, evidently awaiting someone, when I chanced upon it in my extremity.

It is well to take time to consider, when events are of a confusing nature. In that way thoughts are sometimes untangled. Now, in a flash, the truth came to me. Valcour was still at the mansion—Valcour, her accomplice; perhaps her lover.

To realize this evident fact of her intrigue with my brilliant foe sent a shiver through me—a shiver of despair and utter weariness. Still keeping my gaze upon the floor, and noting, half consciously, the click-click of the telegraph instrument, I said:

"Pardon me, donzella, for using your carriage to effect my escape. You see, I have not made an alliance with the royalists, as yet, and my condition is somewhat dangerous. As for the use of your name in my telegram, I have no objection to telling you—now that the message has been sent—that it was a cypher word warning my republican friends of treachery."

"Do you suspect *me* of treachery, Senhor Harcliffe?" she asked in cold, scornful tones.

I looked up, but dropped my eyes again as I confronted the blaze of indignation that flashed from her own.

"I make no accusations, donzella. What is it to me if you Brazilians fight among yourselves for freedom or the Emperor, as it may suit your fancy? I came here to oblige a friend of my father's—the one true man I have found in all your intrigue-ridden country. But he, alas! is dead, and I am powerless to assist farther the cause he loved. So my mission here is ended, and I will go back to America."

Again I looked up; but this time her eyes were lowered and her expression was set and impenetrable.

"Do not let us part in anger," I resumed, a tremor creeping into my voice in spite of me—for this girl had been very dear to my heart. "Let us say we have both acted according to the dictates of conscience, and cherish only memories of the happy days we have passed together, to comfort us in future years."

She started, with upraised hand and eager face half turned toward the door. Far away in the distance I heard the tramp of many hoofs.

"They are coming, senhor!" called the man who stood beside the horses—one of our patriots. "It's the troop of Uruguayans, I am sure."

Pedro, the station-master, ran from his little office and extinguished the one dim lamp that swung from the ceiling of the room in which we stood.

In the darkness that enveloped us Lesba grasped my arm and whispered "Come!" dragging me toward the door. A moment later we were beside the carriage.

"Mount!" she cried, in a commanding voice. "I will ride inside. Take the road to San Tarem. Quick, senhor, as you value *both* our lives!"

I gathered up the reins as Pedro slammed tight the carriage door. A crack of the whip, a shout of encouragement from the two patriots, and we had dashed away upon the dim road leading to the wild, unsettled plains of the North Plateau.

They were good horses. It surprised me to note their mettle and speed, and I guessed they had been carefully chosen for the night's work—an adventure of which this dénouement was scarcely expected. I could see the road but dimly, but I gave the horses slack rein and they sped along at no uncertain pace.

I could no longer hear the hoof-beats of the guards, and judged that either we had outdistanced them or the shrewd Pedro had sent them on a false scent.

Presently the sky brightened, and as the moon shone clear above us I found that we were passing through a rough country that was but sparsely settled. I remembered to have ridden once in this direction with Lesba, but not so far; and the surroundings were therefore strange to me.

For an hour I drove steadily on, and then the girl spoke to me through the open trap in the roof of the carriage.

"A mile or so further will bring us to a fork in the road. Keep to the right," said she.

I returned no answer, although I was burning to question her of many things. But time enough for that, I thought, when we were safely at our journey's end. Indeed, Lesba's mysterious actions—her quick return from Rio in the wake of the Emperor and Valcour, her secret rendezvous in the lane, which I had so suddenly surprised and interrupted, and her evident desire to save me from arrest—all this was not only contradictory to the frank nature of the girl, but to the suspicions I had formed of her betrayal of the conspiracy in co-operation with her treacherous brother.

The key to the mystery was not mine, and I could only wait until Lesba chose to speak and explain her actions.

I came to the fork in the road and turned to the right. The trail— for it had become little more than that—now skirted a heavy growth of underbrush that merged into groves of scattered, stunted trees; and these in time gradually became more compact and stalwart until a great Brazilian forest threw its black shadow over us. Noiselessly the carriage rolled over the beds of moss, which were so thick now that I could scarcely hear a sound of the horses' hoofs, and then I discerned a short distance ahead the outlines of an old, weatherbeaten house.

Lesba had her head through the trap and spoke close to my ear.

"Stop at this place," said she; "for here our journey ends."

I pulled up the horses opposite the dwelling and regarded it somewhat doubtfully. It had been built a hundred yards or so from the edge of the dense forest and seemed utterly deserted. It was a large house, with walls of baked clay and a thatched roof, and its neglected appearance and dreary surroundings gave it a fearsome look as it stood lifeless and weather-stained under the rays of the moon.

"Is the place inhabited?" I asked.

"It must be," she replied. "Go to the door, and knock upon it loudly."

"But the horses—who will mind them, donzella?"

Instantly she scrambled through the trap to the seat beside me and took the reins in her small hands.

"I will look after the horses," said she.

So I climbed down and approached the door. It was sheltered by a rude porch, and flanked upon either side by well-worn benches such as are frequent at wayside inns.

I pounded upon the door and then paused to listen. The sounds drew a hollow reverberation from within, but aroused no other reply.

"Knock again!" called Lesba.

I obeyed, but with no better success. The place seemed uncanny, and I returned abruptly to the carriage, standing beside the wheel and gazing up through the moonlight into the beautiful face the girl bent over me.

"Lesba," said I, pleadingly, "what does all this mean? Why have you brought me to this strange place?"

"To save your life," she answered in a grave voice.

"But how came you to be waiting in the lane? And who were you waiting for?" I persisted.

"By what right do you question me, Senhor Harcliffe?" she asked, drawing back so that I could no longer look into her eyes.

"By no right at all, Lesba. Neither do I care especially whether you are attached to the Empire or the Republic, or how much you indulge in political intrigue, since that appears to be the chief amusement of your countrymen. But I love you. You know it well, although you have never permitted me tell you so. And loving you as I do, with all my heart, I am anxious to untangle this bewildering maze and understand something of your actions since that terrible morning when I parted with you at Dom Miguel's mansion."

She laughed, and the laugh was one of those quaint flashes of merriment peculiar to the girl, leaving one in doubt whether to attribute it to amusement or nervous agitation. Indeed, where another woman might weep Lesba would laugh; so that it frequently puzzled me to comprehend her. Now, however, she surprised me by leaning over me and saying gently:

"I will answer your question, Robert. My brother is at the mansion, and in danger of his life. I was waiting with the carriage to assist him to escape."

"But how do you know he is in danger?"

"He sent me word by a carrier-pigeon."

"To be sure. Yet there is one more thing that troubles me: why were you in Rio, riding in the Emperor's carriage with the spy Valcour?"

"It is simple, senhor. I went to Rio to assist in persuading Dom Pedro to visit the vault."

"Knowing it was empty?"

"Knowing it was empty, and believing that the Emperor's absence would enable Fonseca to strike a blow for freedom."

"Then Fonseca is still faithful to the Cause?"

"I know of no traitor in our ranks, Robert, although it seems you have suspected nearly all of us, at times. But it grows late and my brother is still in peril. Will you again rap upon the door?"

"It is useless, Lesba."

"Try the back door; they may hear you from there," she suggested.

So I made my way, stumbling over tangled vines and protruding roots, to the rear of the house, where the shadows lay even thicker than in front. I found the door, and hammered upon it with all my strength. The noise might have raised the dead, but as I listened intently there came not the least footfall to reward me. For a time I hesitated what to do. From the grim forest behind me I heard a half-audible snarl and the bark of a wolf; in the house an impressive silence reigned supreme.

I drew back, convinced that the place was uninhabited, and returned around the corner of the house.

"There is no one here, donzella," I began, but stopped short in amazement.

The carriage was gone.

XX

"Arise and Strike!"

I sprang to the road and peered eagerly in every direction. Far away in the distance could be discerned the dim outlines of the carriage, flying along the way from whence we had come.

Lesba had brought me to this place only to desert me, and it was not difficult to realize that she had sent me to the rear of the house to get me out of the way while she wheeled the carriage around and dashed away unheard over the soft moss.

Well, I had ceased to speculate upon the girl's erratic actions. Only one thing seemed clear to me; that she had returned to rescue her brother from the danger which threatened him. Why she had assisted me to escape the soldiery only to leave me in this wilderness could be accounted for but by the suggestion that her heart softened toward one whom she knew had learned to love her during those bright days we had passed in each other's society. But that she loved me in return I dared not even hope. Her answer to my declaration had been a laugh, and to me this girl's heart was as a sealed book. Moreover, it occurred to me that Valcour also loved her, and into his eyes I had seen her gaze as she never had gazed into mine during our most friendly intercourse.

The carriage had vanished long since, and the night air was chill. I returned to the porch of the deserted house, and curling myself up on one of the benches soon sank into a profound slumber, for the events of the day had well-nigh exhausted me.

When I awoke a rough-looking, bearded man was bending over me. He wore a peasant's dress and carried a gun on his left arm.

"Who are you, senhor," he demanded, as my eyes unclosed, "and how came you here?"

I arose and stretched myself, considering who he might be.

"Why do you ask?" said I.

"There is war in the land, senhor," he responded, quietly, "and every man must be a friend or a foe to the Republic." He doffed his hat with rude devotion at the word, and added, "Declare yourself, my friend."

I stared at him thoughtfully. War in the land, said he! Then the "torch of rebellion" had really been fired. But by whom? Could it have been Paola, as Valcour had claimed? And why? Since the conspiracy had been unmasked and its leaders, with the exception of Fonseca, either scattered or imprisoned? Did the Minister of Police aim to destroy everyone connected with the Cause by precipitating an impotent revolt? Or was there a master-hand directing these seemingly incomprehensible events?

The man was growing suspicious of my silence.

"Come!" said he, abruptly; "you shall go to Senhor Bastro."

"And where is that?" I asked, with interest, for Paola had reported that Bastro had fled the country.

My captor did not deign to reply. With the muzzle of his gun unpleasantly close to my back he marched me toward the edge of the forest, which we skirted for a time in silence. Then the path turned suddenly into a dense thicket, winding between close-set trees until, deep within the wood, we came upon a natural clearing of considerable extent.

In the center of this space was a large, low building constructed of logs and roofed with branches of trees, and surrounding the entire structure were grouped native Brazilians, armed with rifles, revolvers, and knives.

These men were not uniformed, and their appearance was anything but military; nevertheless there was a look upon their stern faces that warned me they were in deadly earnest and not to be trifled with.

As my intercourse with the republicans had been confined entirely to a few of their leaders, I found no familiar face among these people; so I remained impassive while my captor pushed me past the guards to a small doorway placed near a protecting angle of the building.

"Enter!" said he.

I obeyed, and the next moment stood before a group of men who were evidently the officers or leaders of the little band of armed patriots I had seen without.

"Ah!" said one, in a deep bass voice, "it is Senhor Harcliffe, the secretary to Dom Miguel."

I have before mentioned the fact that whenever the conspirators had visited de Pintra they remained securely masked, so that their features were, with a few exceptions, unknown to me. But the voices were familiar enough, and the man who had brought me here had mentioned Sanchez Bastro's name; so I had little difficulty in guessing the identity of the personage who now addressed me.

"Why are you here, senhor?" he inquired, with evident anxiety; "and do you bring us news of the uprising?"

"I know nothing of the uprising except that your man here," and I turned to my guide, "tells me there is war in the land, and that the Revolution is proclaimed."

"Yes," returned Bastro, with a grave nod.

"Then," I continued, "I advise you to lay down your arms at once and return to your homes before you encounter arrest and imprisonment."

The leaders cast upon one another uneasy looks, and Bastro drew a small paper from his breast and handed it to me. I recognized it as one of the leaves from his note-book which Paola had attached to the carrier-pigeon, and upon it were scrawled these words, "Arise and strike!"

It was the signal long since agreed upon to start the Revolution.

With a laugh I handed back the paper.

"It is from Francisco Paola, the traitor," I said.

"Traitor!" they echoed, in an astonished chorus.

"Listen, gentlemen; it is evident you are ignorant of the events of the last two days." And in as few words as possible I related the occurrences at de Pintra's mansion, laying stress upon the arrest of Piexoto, the perfidy of the Minister of Police, and the death of Treverot.

They were not so deeply impressed as I had expected. The discovery of the empty vault had aroused no interest whatever, and they listened quietly and without comment to my story of Paola's betrayal of his fellow-conspirators to the Emperor.

But when I mentioned Treverot's death Bastro chose to smile, and indicating a tall gentleman standing at his left, he said:

"Permit me to introduce to you Senhor Treverot. He will tell you that he still lives."

"Then Paola lied?" I exclaimed, somewhat chagrined.

Bastro shrugged his shoulders.

"We have confidence in the Minister of Police," said he, calmly. "There is no doubt but General Fonseca, at Rio, has before now gained control of the capital, and that the Revolution is successfully established. We shall know everything very soon, for my men have gone to the nearest telegraph station for news. Meantime, to guard against any emergency, our patriots are being armed in readiness for combat, and, in Matto Grosso at least, the royalists are powerless to oppose us."

"But the funds—the records! What will happen if the Emperor seizes them?" I asked.

"The Emperor will not seize them," returned Bastro, unmoved. "The contents of the vault are in safe-keeping."

Before I could question him further a man sprang through the doorway.

"The wires from Rio are cut in every direction," said he, in an agitated voice. "A band of the Uruguayan guards, under de Souza and Valcour, is galloping over the country to arrest every patriot they can find, and our people are hiding themselves in terror."

Consternation spread over the features of the little band which a moment before had deemed itself so secure and powerful. Bastro turned to pace the earthen floor with anxious strides, while the others watched him silently.

"What of Francisco Paola?" suddenly asked the leader.

"Why, senhor, he seems to have disappeared," replied the scout, with hesitation.

"Disappeared! And why?"

"Perhaps I can answer that question, Senhor Bastro," said a voice behind us, and turning my head I saw my friend Pedro, the station-master at Cuyaba, standing within the doorway.

"Enter, Pedro," commanded the leader. "What news do you bring, and why have you abandoned your post?"

"The wires are down," said the station-master, "and no train is allowed to leave Rio since the Emperor reached there at midnight."

"Then you know nothing of what has transpired at the capital?" asked Bastro.

"Nothing, senhor. It was yesterday morning when the Emperor's party met the train at Cuyaba, and I handed him a telegram from de Lima, the Minister of State. It read in this way: 'General Fonseca and his army have revolted and seized the palace, the citadel, and all public buildings. I have called upon every loyal Brazilian to rally to the support of the Empire. Return at once. Arrest the traitors Francisco Paola and his sister. Situation critical."

"Ah!" cried Bastro, drawing a deep breath, "and what said the Emperor to that message?"

"He spoke with his counselors, and wired this brief reply to de Lima, 'I am coming.' Also he sent a soldier back to de Pintra's mansion with orders to arrest Francisco and Lesba Paola. Then he boarded the train and instructed the conductor to proceed to Rio with all possible haste. And that is all I know, senhor, save that I called up Rio last evening and learned that Fonseca was still in control of the city. At midnight the wires were cut and nothing further can be learned. Therefore I came to join you, and if there is a chance to fight for the Cause I beg that you will accept my services."

Bastro paused in his walk to press the honest fellow's hand; then he resumed his thoughtful pacing.

The others whispered among themselves, and one said:

"Why need we despair, Sanchez Bastro? Will not Fonseca, once in control, succeed in holding the city?"

"Surely!" exclaimed the leader. "It is not for him that I fear, but for ourselves. If the Uruguayans are on our trail we must disperse our men and scatter over the country, for the spy Valcour knows, I am sure, of this rendezvous."

"But they are not hunting you, senhor," protested Pedro, "but rather Paola and his sister, who have managed to escape from de Pintra's house."

"Nevertheless, the Uruguayans are liable to be here at any moment," returned Bastro, "and there is nothing to be gained by facing that devil, de Souza."

He then called his men together in the clearing, explained to them the situation, and ordered them to scatter and to secrete themselves in the edges of the forests and pick off the Uruguayans with their rifles whenever occasion offered.

"If anything of importance transpires," he added, "report to me at once at my house."

Without a word of protest his commands were obeyed. The leaders mounted their horses and rode away through the numerous forest paths that led into the clearing.

The men also saluted and disappeared among the trees, and presently only Bastro, Pedro, and myself stood in the open space. "Come with me, Senhor Harcliffe," said the leader; "I shall be glad to have you join me at breakfast. You may follow us, Pedro."

Then he strode to the edge of the clearing, pressed aside some bushes, and stepped into a secret path that led through the densest portion of the tangled forest. I followed, and Pedro brought up the rear.

For some twenty minutes Bastro guided us along the path, which might well have been impassable to a novice, until finally we emerged from the forest to find the open country before us, and a small, cozy-looking dwelling facing us from the opposite side of a well-defined roadway.

Bastro led us to a side door, which he threw open, and then stepped back with a courteous gesture.

"Enter, gentlemen," said he; "you are welcome to my humble home."

I crossed the threshold and came to an abrupt stop. Something seemed to clutch my heart with a grip of iron; my limbs trembled involuntarily, and my eyes grew set and staring.

For, standing before me, with composed look and a smile upon his dark face, was the living form of my lamented friend Miguel de Pintra!

XXI

One Mystery Solved

C ompose yourself, my dear Robert," said Dom Miguel, pressing my hands in both his own. "It is no ghost you see, for—thanks be to God!—I am still alive."

I had no words to answer him. In all my speculations as to the result of Madam Izabel's terrible deed, the fate of the records and the mysterious opening of the vault without its key, I never had conceived the idea that Dom Miguel might have escaped his doom. And to find him here, not only alive, but apparently in good health and still busy with the affairs of the Revolution, conveyed so vivid a shock to my nerves that I could but dumbly stare into my old friend's kind eyes and try to imagine that I beheld a reality and not the vision of a disordered brain.

Bastro assisted me by laughing loudly and giving me a hearty slap across the shoulders.

"Wake up, Senhor Harcliffe!" said he; "and hereafter have more faith in Providence and the luck that follows in the wake of true patriotism. We could ill afford to lose our chief at this juncture."

"But how did it happen?" I gasped, still filled with wonder. "What earthly power could have opened that awful vault when its key was miles and miles away?"

"The earthly power was wielded by a very ordinary little woman," said Dom Miguel, with his old gentle smile. "When you rode away from the house on that terrible morning Lesba came and unlocked my prison, setting me free."

"But how?" I demanded, still blindly groping for the truth.

"By means of a duplicate key that she had constantly carried in her bosom."

I drew a long breath.

"Did you know of this key, sir?" I asked, after a pause, which my companions courteously forbore to interrupt.

"I did not even suspect its existence," replied Dom Miguel. "But it seems that Francisco Paola, with his usual thoughtfulness, took an impression in wax of my ring, without my knowledge, and had an exact duplicate prepared. I think he foresaw that an emergency might arise when another key might be required; but it would not do to let anyone know of his action, for the mere knowledge that such a duplicate existed would render us all suspicious and uneasy. So he kept the matter secret even from me, and gave the ring into the keeping of his sister, who was his only confidante, and whom he had requested me to accept as an inmate of my household, under the plea that I am her legal guardian. This was done in order to have her always at hand in case the interests of the conspiracy demanded immediate use of the duplicate key. That Francisco trusted her more fully than he has any other living person is obvious; and that she was worthy of such trust the girl has fully proved."

"Then you were released at once?" I asked; "and you suffered little from your confinement?"

"My anguish was more mental than of a bodily nature," Dom Miguel answered, sadly; "but I was free to meet Paola when he arrived at my house, and to assist him and Lesba in removing the contents of the vault to a safer place."

"But why, knowing that his sister held a duplicate key, did the Minister send me in chase of the ring Madam Izabel had stolen?" I demanded.

"Because it was necessary to keep the matter from the Emperor until the records had been removed," explained de Pintra. "Indeed, Francisco was on his way to us that morning to insist upon our abandoning the vault, after having given us warning, as you will remember, the night before, that the clever hiding-place of our treasure and papers was no longer a secret."

"I remember that he himself revealed the secret to the Emperor," I remarked, dryly.

"And acted wisely in doing so, I have no doubt," retorted Bastro, who still stood beside us. "But come, gentlemen, breakfast must be ready, and I have a vigorous appetite. Be good enough to join me."

He led the way to an inner room, and de Pintra and I followed, his arm in mine.

It seemed to me, now that I regarded him more attentively, that my old friend was less erect than formerly, that there were new and deep furrows upon his gentle face, and that his eyes had grown dim and sunken. But that the old, dauntless spirit remained I never doubted.

As we entered the breakfast-room I saw a form standing at the window—the form of a little man clothed neatly in black. He turned to greet us with pale, expressionless features and drooping eyelids.

It was Captain Mazanovitch.

"Good morning, Senhor Harcliffe," he said, in his soft voice; and I wondered how he had recognized me without seeming to open his eyes. "And what news does our noble Captain Bastro bring of the Revolution?" he continued, with a slight note of interest in his voice that betrayed his eagerness.

While we breakfasted Bastro related the events of the morning, and told how the news he had received of the activity of the Uruguayan guards, in connection with the impossibility of learning from Rio what Fonseca had accomplished, had induced him to disband his men.

"But can you again assemble them, if you should wish to?" inquired Dom Miguel.

"Easily," answered our host; but he did not explain how.

While he and Dom Miguel discussed the fortunes of the Revolution I made bold to ask Captain Mazanovitch how he came to be in this isolated spot.

"I was warned by the Minister of Police to leave Rio," answered the detective; "for it appears my—my friend Valcour would have been suspicious had not Paola promised to arrest me with the others. I have been here since yesterday."

"Your friend Valcour is a most persistent foe to the Cause," said I, thoughtfully. "It would have pleased you to watch him struggle with Paola for the mastery, while the Emperor was by. Ah, how Paola and Valcour hate each other!"

Mazanovitch turned his passionless face toward me, and it seemed as though a faint smile flickered for an instant around his mouth. But he made no answer.

After breakfast Pedro was sent back to Cuyaba for news, being instructed to await there the repairing of the telegraph wires, and to communicate with us as soon as he had word from Rio.

The man had no sooner disappeared in the forest than, as we stood in the roadway looking after him, a far-off patter of horses' feet was distinctly heard approaching from the north.

Silently we stood, gazing toward the curve in the road while the hoof-beats grew louder and louder, till suddenly two horses swept around the edge of the forest and bore down upon us.

Then to the surprise of all we recognized the riders to be Francisco Paola and his sister Lesba, and they rode the same horses which the evening before had been attached to the carriage that had brought me from de Pintra's.

As they dashed up both brother and sister sprang from the panting animals, and the former said, hurriedly:

"Quick, comrades! Into the house and barricade the doors. The Uruguayans are upon us!"

True enough; now that their own horses had come to a halt we plainly heard the galloping of the troop of pursuers. With a single impulse we ran to the house and entered, when my first task was to assist Bastro in placing the shutters over the windows and securing them with stout bars.

The doors were likewise fastened and barred, and then Mazanovitch brought us an armful of rifles and an ample supply of ammunition.

"Do you think it wise to resist?" asked de Pintra, filling with cartridges the magazine of a rifle.

A blow upon the door prevented an answer.

"Open, in the name of the Emperor!" cried an imperious voice.

"That is my gallant friend Captain de Souza," said Lesba, with a little laugh.

I looked at the strange girl curiously. She had seated herself upon a large chest, and with her hands clasped about one knee was watching us load our weapons with as much calmness as if no crisis of our fate was impending.

"Be kind to him, Lesba," remarked Paola, tucking a revolver underneath his arm while he rolled and lighted a cigarette. "Think of his grief at being separated from you."

She laughed again, with real enjoyment, and shook the tangled locks of hair from her eyes.

"Perhaps if I accept his attentions he will marry me, and I shall escape," she rejoined, lightly.

"Open, I command you!" came the voice from without.

"Really," said Lesba, looking upon us brightly, "it was too funny for anything. Twice this morning the brave captain nearly succeeded in capturing me. He might have shot me with ease, but called out that he could not bear to injure the woman he loved!"

"Does he indeed love you, Lesba?" asked de Pintra, gently.

"So he says, Uncle. But it must have been a sudden inspiration, for I never saw him until yesterday."

"Nevertheless, I am glad to learn of this," resumed Dom Miguel; "for there is no disguising the fact that they outnumber us and are better armed, and it is good to know that whatever happens to us, you will be protected."

"Whatever happens to you will happen to me," declared the girl, springing to her feet. "Give me a gun, Uncle!"

Now came another summons from de Souza.

"Listen!" he called; "the house is surrounded and you cannot escape us. Therefore it will be well for you to surrender and rely upon the Emperor's mercy."

"I fear we may not rely on that with any security," drawled Paola, who had approached the door. "Pray tell us, my good de Souza, what are your orders respecting us?"

"To arrest you at all hazards," returned the captain, sternly.

"And then?" persisted the Minister, leaning against the door and leisurely puffing his cigarette.

But another voice was now heard—Valcour's—crying:

"Open at once, or we will batter down the door."

Before any could reply Mazanovitch pushed Paola aside and placed his lips to the keyhole.

"Hear me, Valcour," he said, in a soft yet penetrating tone, "we are able to defend ourselves until assistance arrives. But rather than that blood should be shed without necessity, we will surrender ourselves if we have your assurance of safe convoy to Rio."

For a moment there was silence. Then, "How came *you* here?" demanded the spy, in accents that betrayed his agitation.

"That matters little," returned Mazanovitch. "Have we your assurance of safety?"

We heard the voices of Valcour and de Souza in angry dispute; then the captain shouted: "Stand aside!" and there came a furious blow upon the door that shattered the panels.

Bastro raised his rifle and fired. A cry answered the shot, but instantly a second crash followed. The bars were torn from their sockets, the splintered door fell inward, and before we could recover from the surprise we were looking into the muzzles of a score of carbines leveled upon us.

"Very well," said Paola, tossing the end of his cigarette through the open doorway. "We are prisoners of war. Peste! my dear Captain; how energetic your soldiers are!"

A moment later we were disarmed, and then, to our surprise, de Souza ordered our feet and our hands to be securely bound. Only Lesba escaped this indignity, for the captain confined her in a small room adjoining our own and placed a guard at the door.

During this time Valcour stood by, sullen and scowling, his hands clinched nervously and his lips curling with scorn.

"You might gag us, my cautious one," said Paola, addressing the officer, who had planted himself, stern and silent, in the center of the room while his orders were being executed.

"So I will, Senhor Paola; but in another fashion," was the grim reply.

He drew a paper from his breast and continued, "I will read to you my orders from his Majesty, the Emperor Dom Pedro of Brazil, dispatched from the station at Cuyaba as he was departing for his capital to quell the insurrection."

He paused and slowly unfolded the paper, while every eye—save that, perhaps, of Mazanovitch—was fixed upon him with intent gaze.

"'You are instructed to promptly arrest the traitor Francisco Paola, together with his sister, Lesba Paola, and whatever revolutionists you may be able to take, and to execute them one and all without formal trial on the same day that they are captured, as enemies of the Empire and treasonable conspirators plotting the downfall of the Government.'"

The captain paused a moment, impressively, and refolded the document.

"It is signed by his Majesty's own hand, and sealed with the royal seal," he said.

XXII

The Death Sentence

I glanced around the room to note the effect of this startling announcement upon my fellow-prisoners. Bastro's scowling face was turned full upon the officer, but showed no sign of fear. De Pintra smiled rather scornfully and whispered a word to Mazanovitch, whose countenance remained impassive as ever. Paola, with the perpetual simper distorting his naturally handsome features, leaned back in his chair and regarded his trussed ankles with whimsical indifference. Indeed, if the captain thought to startle or terrify his captives he must have been grievously disappointed, for one and all received the announcement of the death sentence with admirable composure.

It was Valcour who broke the silence. Confronting the captain with blazing eyes, while his slight form quivered with excitement, he cried:

"This is nonsense, de Souza! The Emperor must have been mad to write such an order. You will convey your prisoners to Rio for trial."

"I shall obey the Emperor's commands," answered the captain, gloomily.

"But it is murder!"

"It is the Emperor's will."

"Hear me, Captain de Souza," said Valcour, drawing himself up proudly; "you were instructed to obey my commands. I order you to convey the prisoners to Rio, that they may be tried in a court of justice."

The other shook his head.

"The order is to me personally, and I must obey. A soldier never questions the commands of his superiors."

"But I am your superior!"

"Not in this affair, Senhor Valcour. And the Emperor's order is doubtless to be obeyed above that of his spy."

Valcour winced, and turned away to pace the floor nervously.

"But the lady—surely you will not execute the Donzella Paola in this brutal fashion!" he protested, after an interval of silence.

The captain flushed, and then grew pale.

"I will speak with the lady," he said, and motioning aside the guard he entered the room where Lesba was confined, and closed the door after him.

We could hear his voice through the thin partition, speaking in low and earnest tones. Then a burst of merry laughter from Lesba fell upon our ears with something of a shock, for the matter seemed serious enough to insure gravity. Evidently the captain protested, but the girl's high-pitched tones and peals of merriment indicated that she was amusing herself at his expense, and suddenly the door burst open and de Souza stumbled out with a red and angry face.

"The woman is a fiend!" he snarled. "Let her die with the others."

Valcour, who had continued to pace the floor during this interview, had by now managed to get his nerves under control, for he smiled at the captain, and said:

"Let us see if I have any argument that will avail."

While the officer stood irresolute, Valcour bowed mockingly, opened the door, and passed into Lesba's room.

It was de Souza's turn now to pace the floor, which he did with slow and measured strides; but although we strained our ears, not a sound of the interview that was progressing reached us through the partition.

After a considerable time it seemed that the captain regretted having allowed Valcour this privilege, for he advanced to the door and placed his hand on the knob. Instantly the spy appeared, closing the door swiftly behind him and turning the key in the lock.

"I withdraw my opposition, Captain," said he. "You may execute the lady with the others, for all I care. When is the massacre to take place?"

The officer stroked his moustache and frowned.

"The order commands the execution on the same day the conspirators are arrested," he announced. "I do not like the job, Valcour, believe me; but the Emperor must be obeyed. Let them die at sunset."

He turned abruptly and left the house, but sent a detachment of the Uruguayans to remain in the room with us and guard against any attempt on our part to escape.

We indulged in little conversation. Each had sufficient to occupy his thoughts, and sunset was not very far away, after all. To me this ending of the bold conspiracy was not surprising, for I had often thought that when Dom Pedro chose to strike he would strike in a way that would deter all plotting against the government for sometime to come. And life is of little value in these South American countries.

"Where are the records?" I whispered to Dom Miguel, who sat near me.

"Safe with Fonseca in Rio," he answered.

"Do you imagine that Fonseca will succeed?" I continued.

"He is sure to," said the chief, a soft gleam lighting his eyes. "It is only we who have failed, my friend." He paused a moment, and then resumed: "I am sorry I have brought you to this, Robert. For the rest of us it matters little that we die. Is not a free Brazil a glorious prize to be won by the purchase of a few lives?"

It was futile to answer. A free Brazil meant little to me, I reflected; but to die with Lesba was a bit comforting, after all. I must steel myself to meet death as bravely as this girl was sure to do.

Paola, after sitting long silent, addressed Valcour, who, since the captain's exit, had been staring from the window that faced the forest.

"What did de Souza say to Lesba?" he asked.

The spy turned around with a countenance more composed and cheerful than he had before shown, and answered:

"He offered to save her from death if she would marry him."

"Ah; and she laughed at the dear captain, as we all heard. But you, senhor, made an effort to induce her to change her mind—did you not?"

"I?" returned Valcour. "By no means, senhor. It is better she should die than marry this brutal Captain de Souza."

This speech seemed to confirm my suspicion that Valcour himself loved Lesba. But Paola cast one of his quick, searching glances into the spy's face and seemed pleased by what he discovered there.

"May I speak with my sister?" he asked, a moment later.

"Impossible, senhor. She must remain in solitary confinement until the hour of execution, for the captain's gallantry will not permit him to bind her."

Then, approaching de Pintra, Valcour stood a moment looking down at him and said:

"Sir, you have made a noble fight for a cause that has doubtless been very dear to you. And you have lost. In these last hours that you are permitted to live will you not make a confession to your Emperor, and give him the details of that conspiracy in which you were engaged?"

"In Rio," answered Dom Miguel, quietly, "there is now no Emperor. The Republic is proclaimed. Even at this moment the people of our country are acclaiming the United States of Brazil. Senhor, your power is ended. You may, indeed, by your master's orders, murder us in this faraway province before assistance can reach us. But our friends will exact a terrible vengeance for the deed, be assured."

Valcour did not answer at once. He stood for a time with knitted brows, thoughtfully regarding the white-haired chieftain of the Republic, whose brave utterances seemed to us all to be fraught with prophetic insight.

"If your lives were in my hands," said the spy, with a gesture of weariness, "you would be tried in a court of justice. I am no murderer, senhor, and I sincerely grieve that de Souza should consider his orders positive."

He turned abruptly to Mazanovitch, and throwing an arm around the little man's shoulders bent swiftly down and pressed a kiss upon the pallid forehead. Then, with unsteady gait he walked from the room, and at last I saw the eyes of Mazanovitch open wide, a gaze of ineffable tenderness following the retreating form, until Valcour had disappeared. Paola also was staring, and the disgusting simper had left his face, for a time, at least.

Silence now fell upon the room. Bastro, in his corner, had gone to sleep, and Dom Miguel seemed lost in thought. From the chamber in which Lesba was confined came no sound to denote whether the girl grieved over her approaching fate or bore it with the grim stoicism of her doomed comrades.

The guard paced up and down before the closed door, pausing at times to mutter a word to his fellows, who stood watchfully over us. From my station on the chest I could gaze into the yard and note the shadow of the house creeping further and further out into the sunshine, bringing ever nearer the hour when the bright orb would sink into the far-away plateau and our eyes would be closed forever in death.

Yet the time dragged wearily, it seemed to me. When one is condemned to die it is better to suffer quickly, and have done with it. To wait, to count the moments, is horrible. One needs to have nerves of iron to endure that.

Nevertheless, we endured it. The hours passed, somehow, and the shadows grew dim with stretching.

Suddenly I heard a clank of spurs as de Souza approached. He gave a brief order to the Uruguayans who were lounging in the yard, and then stepped through the doorway and faced us.

"Get ready, senhors," said he. "The hour has come."

XXIII

AT THE ELEVENTH HOUR

We aroused ourselves, at this, and regarded the captain attentively. He turned his stern gaze upon one after the other, and gave a growl of satisfaction as he noted no craven amongst us.

"You shall draw cuts, gentlemen, to decide the order in which you must expiate your crime. I will show no partiality. See, here are the slips, a number written upon each. Julio shall place them in his hat and allow you to draw."

He handed the bits of paper to one of his men and strode to the door of Lesba's room.

"Open!" he commanded, giving it a rap with his knuckles.

There was no reply.

"Open!" said he, again, and placed his ear to the panel.

Then, with a sudden gesture, he swung the door inward.

A moment the officer stood motionless, gazing into the chamber. Then he turned to us a face convulsed with anger.

"Who permitted the woman to escape?" he demanded.

The guards, startled and amazed, peered over his shoulders into the vacant room; but none dared to answer.

"What now, Captain, has your bird flown?" came Valcour's soft voice, and the spy entered the room and threw himself carelessly into a chair.

De Souza looked upon his colleague with evident suspicion, and twisted the ends of his moustache in sullen fury. Perhaps he dared not accuse Valcour openly, as the latter was the Emperor's authorized representative. And it may be the captain was not sincerely sorry that Lesba had escaped, and so saved him from the necessity of executing her, for, after a period of indecision, the wrath of the officer seemed to cool, and he slowly regained his composure. Valcour, who was watching him, appeared to notice this, and said:

"You forgot the window, my Captain. It was not difficult for the senhorita to steal across the roadway unobserved and take refuge in the forest. For my part, I am glad she is gone. Our royal master has little credit in condemning a woman to such a death."

L. FRANK BAUM

"Have a care, senhor! Your words are treasonable."

"The Emperor will be the first to applaud them, when he has time to think. Indeed, de Souza, were I in your place, I should ignore the order to execute these people. His Majesty acted under a severe nervous strain, and he will not thank you, believe me, for carrying out his instructions so literally."

"A soldier's duty is to obey," returned the officer, stiffly. Then, turning to the tall Uruguayan who held the hat, he added:

"Let the prisoners draw, Julio!"

Another soldier now unfastened our bonds, and Paola, who was the first to be approached by Julio, took a slip of paper from the hat and thrust it into his pocket without examination.

Sanchez Bastro drew next, and smiled as he read his number. Then came my turn, and I own that I could not repress a slight trembling of my fingers as I drew forth the fatal slip. It was number four.

"Good!" murmured de Pintra, reading the slip over my shoulder. "I shall not be alive to witness your death, Robert." And then he took the last paper from the hat and added: "I am number two."

"I am first," said Bastro, with cheerfulness. "It is an honor, Dom Miguel," and he bowed respectfully to the chief.

Paola wore again the old, inane smile that always lent his face an indescribable leer of idiocy. I knew, by this time, that the expression was indeed a mask to cover his real feelings, and idly wondered if he would choose to die with that detestable simper upon his lips.

"Come, gentlemen; we are ready."

It was the captain who spoke, and we rose obediently and filed through the doorway, closely guarded by the Uruguayans.

In the vacant space that served as a yard for Bastro's house stood a solitary date-palm with a straight, slender trunk. Before this we halted, and Bastro was led to the tree and a rope passed around his body securing him to the trunk. They offered to blindfold him, but he waved the men aside.

"It will please me best to look into the muzzles of your guns," said the patriot, in a quiet voice. "I am not afraid, Senhor Captain."

De Souza glanced at the sun. It was slowly sinking, a ball of vivid red, into the bosom of the far-away plateau.

At a gesture from the officer six of the guardsmen stepped forward and leveled their carbines upon Bastro, who stood upright against the tree, with a proud smile upon his manly face.

I turned away my head, feeling sick and dizzy; and the rattle of carbines set me trembling with nervous horror. Nor did I look toward the tree again, although, after an interval of silence, I heard the tramp of soldiers bearing Bastro's body to the deserted house.

"Number two!" cried de Souza, harshly.

It was no time to turn craven. My own death was but a question of moments, and I realized that I had little time to bid farewell to my kind friend and strive to cheer him upon his way. Going to his side I seized Dom Miguel's hand and pressed it to my lips; but he was not content with that, and caught me in a warm and affectionate embrace.

Then he was led to the tree. I turned my back, covering my face with my hands.

"For the Cause!" I heard his gentle voice say. The carbines rang out again, and a convulsive sob burst from my throat in spite of my strong efforts to control my emotion.

Again I listened to the solemn tread of the soldiers, while from far away the sound of a shout was borne to us upon the still evening air.

Somehow, that distant shout thrilled me with a new-born hope, and I gazed eagerly along the line of roadway that skirted the forest.

De Souza was gazing there, too, with a disturbed look upon his face; but the light was growing dim, and we could see nothing.

"Number three!"

It was Paola's turn, and he walked unassisted to the tree and set his back to it, while the soldiers passed the rope under his arms and then retired. But they left Valcour confronting the prisoner, and I saw the simper fade from Paola's lips and an eager gleam light his pale features.

For a few moments they stood thus, separated from all the rest, and exchanging earnest whispers, while the captain stamped his foot with savage impatience.

"Come, come, Valcour!" he called, at last. "You are interfering with my duty. Leave the prisoner, I command you!"

The spy turned around, and his face was positively startling in its expression of intense agony.

"If you are in a hurry, my dear Captain, fire upon us both!" said he, bitterly.

With a muttered oath de Souza strode forward, and seizing Valcour by the arm, dragged him back of the firing-line.

But at that instant a startling sound reached our ears—the sound of a cheer—and with it came the rapid patter of horses' feet.

The soldiers, who had already leveled their guns at Paola, swung suddenly around upon their heels; de Souza uttered an exclamation of dismay, and the rest of us stood as motionless as if turned to stone.

For sweeping around the curve of the forest came a troop of horsemen, led by a girl whose fluttering white skirts trailed behind her like a banner borne on the breeze. God! how they rode—the horses plunging madly forward at every bound, their red eyes and distended nostrils bearing evidence of the wild run that had well-nigh exhausted their strength.

And the riders, as they sighted us, screamed curses and encouragement in the same breath, bearing down upon our silent group with the speed of a whirlwind.

There was little time for the Uruguayans to recover from their surprise, for at close range the horsemen let fly a volley from rifle and revolver that did deadly havoc. A few saddles were emptied in return, but almost instantly the soldiers and patriots were engaged in a desperate hand-to-hand conflict, with no quarter given or expected.

De Souza fell wounded at the first volley, and I saw Valcour, with a glad cry, start forward and run toward Paola, who was still bound to his tree. But the captain, half raising himself from the ground, aimed his revolver at the prisoner, as if determined upon his death in spite of the promised rescue.

"Look out!" I shouted, observing the action.

Paola was, of course, helpless to evade the bullet; but Valcour, who had nearly reached him, turned suddenly at my cry and threw himself in front of Paola just as the shot rang out.

An instant the spy stood motionless. Then, tossing his arms above his head, he fell backward and lay still.

XXIV

The Emperor's Spy

Although the deadly conflict was raging all about us, I passed it by to regard a still more exciting tragedy. For with a roar like that from a mad bull Mazanovitch dashed aside his captors and sprang to the spot where Valcour lay.

"Oh, my darling, my darling!" he moaned, raising the delicate form that he might pillow the head upon his knee. "How dared they harm you, my precious one! How dared they!"

Paola, struggling madly with his bonds, succeeded in bursting them asunder, and now staggered up to kneel beside Valcour. His eyes were staring and full of a horror that his own near approach to death had never for an instant evoked.

Taking one of the spy's slender hands in both his own he pressed it to his heart and said in trembling tones:

"Look up, sweetheart! Look up, I beg of you. It is Francisco—do you not know me? Are you dead, Valcour? Are you dead?"

A gentle hand pushed him aside, and Lesba knelt in his place. With deft fingers she bared Valcour's breast, tearing away the soft linen through which a crimson stain had already spread, and bending over a wound in the left shoulder to examine it closely. Standing beside the little group, I found myself regarding the actors in this remarkable drama with an interest almost equaling their own. The bared breast revealed nothing to me, however; for already I knew that Valcour was a woman.

Presently Lesba looked up into the little man's drawn face and smiled.

"Fear nothing, Captain Mazanovitch," said she softly; "the wound is not very dangerous, and—please God!—we will yet save your daughter's life."

His daughter! How much of the mystery that had puzzled me this simple word revealed!

Paola, still kneeling and covering his face with his hands, was sobbing like a child; Mazanovitch drew a long breath and allowed his lids to again droop slowly over his eyes; and then Lesba looked up and our eyes met.

"I am just in time, Robert," she murmured happily, and bent over Valcour to hide the flush that dyed her sweet face.

I started, and looked around me. In the gathering twilight the forms of the slaughtered Uruguayans lay revealed where they had fallen, for not a single member of Dom Pedro's band of mercenaries had escaped the vengeance of the patriots.

Those of our rescuers who survived were standing in a little group near by, leaning upon their long rifles, awaiting further commands.

Among them I recognized Pedro, and beckoning him to follow me I returned to the house and lifted a door from its hinges. Between us we bore it to the yard and very gently placed Valcour's slight form upon the improvised stretcher.

She moaned at the movement, slowly unclosing her eyes. It was Paola's face that bent over her and Paola that pressed her hand; so she smiled and closed her eyes again, like a tired child.

We carried her into the little chamber from whence Lesba had escaped, for in the outer room lay side by side the silent forms of the martyrs of the Republic.

Tenderly placing Valcour upon the couch, Pedro and I withdrew and closed the door behind us.

I had started to pass through the outer room into the yard when an exclamation from the station-master arrested me. Turning back I found that Pedro had knelt beside Dom Miguel and with broken sobs was pressing the master's hand passionately to his lips. My own heart was heavy with sorrow as I leaned over the outstretched form of our beloved chief for a last look into his still face.

Even as I did so my pulse gave a bound of joy. The heavy eyelids trembled—ever so slightly—the chest expanded in a gentle sigh, and slowly—oh, so slowly!—the eyes of Dom Miguel unclosed and gazed upon us with their accustomed sweetness and intelligence.

"Master! Master!" cried Pedro, bending over with trembling eagerness, "it is done! It is done, my master! The Revolution is accomplished— Fonseca is supreme in Rio—the army is ours! The country is ours! God bless the Republic of Brazil!"

My own heart swelled at the glad tidings, now heard for the first time. But over the face of the martyred chief swept an expression of joy so ecstatic—so like a dream of heaven fulfilled—that we scarcely breathed as we watched the light grow radiant in his eyes and linger there while an ashen pallor succeeded the flush upon his cheeks.

Painfully Dom Miguel reached out his arms to us, and Pedro and I each clasped a hand within our own.

"I am glad," he whispered, softly. "Glad and content. God bless the Republic of Brazil!"

The head fell back; the light faded from his eyes and left them glazed and staring; a tremor passed through his body, communicating its agony even to us who held his hands, as by an electric current.

Pedro still kneeled and sobbed, but I contented myself with pressing the hand and laying it gently upon Dom Miguel's breast.

Truly it was done, and well done. In Rio they were cheering the Republic, while here in this isolated cottage, surrounded by the only carnage the Revolution had involved, lay stilled forever that great heart which had given to its native land the birthright of Liberty.

LESBA HAD DRESSED VALCOUR'S WOUND with surprising skill, and throughout the long, dreary night she bathed the girl's hot forehead and nursed her as tenderly as a sister might, while Paola sat silently by and watched her every movement.

In the early morning Pedro summoned us to breakfast, which he had himself prepared; and, as Valcour was sleeping, Lesba and Mazanovitch joined me at the table while Paola still kept ward in the wounded girl's chamber.

The patriots were digging a trench in which to inter the dead Uruguayans, and I stood in the doorway a moment and watched them, drinking in at the same time the cool morning air.

There Lesba joined me, somewhat pale from her night's watching, and although as yet no word of explanation had passed between us, she knew that I no longer doubted her loyalty, and forbore to blame me for my stupidity in not comprehending that her every action had been for the welfare of the Cause.

At breakfast Pedro told us more of the wonderful news; how the Revolution had succeeded in Rio with practically no bloodshed or resistance; how Fonseca had met the Emperor at the train on his arrival and escorted him, well guarded, to the port, where he was put on board a ship that sailed at once for Lisbon. Indeed, that was to be the last of Dom Pedro's rule, for the populace immediately proclaimed Fonseca dictator, and the patriots' dream of a Republic of Brazil had become an established fact.

Presently we passed into the outer room and looked upon the still form of Miguel de Pintra, the man to whose genius the new Republic owed its success—the great leader who had miserably perished on the very eve of his noble achievement.

The conspiracy was a conspiracy no longer; it had attained to the dignity of a masterly Revolution, and the Cause of Freedom had once more prevailed!

Taking Lesba's hand we passed the bodies of Bastro and Captain de Souza and gained the yard, walking slowly along the road that skirted the forest, while she told me how Valcour had assisted her to escape from the chamber, that she might summon the patriots to effect our rescue. She had wandered long in the forest, she explained, before Pedro met her and assisted her to gather the band that had saved us. Yet the brave girl's grief was intense that she had not arrived in time to rescue her guardian, Dom Miguel, whom she so dearly loved.

"Yet I think, Robert," said she, with tearful eyes, "that uncle would have died willingly had he known the Republic was assured."

"He did know it," said I. "For a moment, last evening, he recovered consciousness. It was but a moment, but long enough for Pedro to tell him the glorious news of victory. And he died content, Lesba, although I know how happy it would have made him to live to see the triumph of the new Republic. His compatriots would also have taken great pride in honoring Dom Miguel above all men for his faithful service."

She made no reply to this, and for a time we walked on in gloomy silence.

"Tell me, Lesba, have you long had knowledge of Valcour's real identity?"

"Francisco told me the truth months ago, and that he loved her," she replied. "But Valcour was sworn to the Emperor's service, and would not listen to my brother as long as she suspected him of being in league with the Republicans. So they schemed and struggled against one another for the supremacy, while each admired the other's talents, and doubtless longed for the warfare to cease."

"And how came this girl to be the Emperor's spy, masquerading under the guise of a man?" I inquired.

"She is the daughter of Captain Mazanovitch, who, when her mother died, took delight in instructing his child in all the arts known to the detective police. As she grew up she became of great service to her father, being often employed upon missions of extreme delicacy and even danger. Mazanovitch used to boast that she was a better detective than himself, and the Emperor became attached to the girl and made her his confidential body-guard, sending her at times upon important secret missions connected with the government. When Mazanovitch was won over to the Republican conspiracy his daughter, whose real name is Carlotta, refused to desert the Emperor, and from that time on treated her father as a traitor, and opposed her wit to his own on every occasion. The male attire she wore both for convenience and as a disguise; but I have learned to know Valcour well, and have found her exceedingly sweet and womanly, despite her professional calling."

It was all simple enough, once one had the clew; yet so extraordinary was the story that it aroused my wonder. In no other country than half-civilized Brazil, I reflected, could such a drama have been enacted.

When we returned to the house we passed the window of Valcour's room and paused to look through the open sash.

The girl was awake and apparently much better, for she smiled brightly into the face Paola bent over her, and showed no resentment when he stooped to kiss her lips.

XXV

The Girl I Love

It was long ago, that day that brought Liberty to Brazil and glory to the name of Miguel de Pintra. Fate is big, but her puppets are small, and such atoms are easily swept aside and scattered by the mighty flood-tide of events for which we hold capricious Fate responsible.

Yet they leave records, these atoms.

I remember how we came to Rio—Valcour, Lesba, Paola, and I—and how Paola was carried through the streets perched upon the shoulders of the free citizens, while vast throngs pressed around to cheer and strong men struggled to touch the patriot's hand and load him with expressions of love and gratitude. And there was no simper upon Paola's face then, you may be sure. Since the tragedy at Bastro's that disagreeable expression had vanished forever, to be replaced by a manliness that was the fellow's most natural attribute, and fitted his fine features much better than the repulsive leer he had formerly adopted as a mask.

Valcour, still weak, but looking rarely beautiful in her womanly robes, rode in a carriage beside Francisco and shared in the fullness of his triumph. The patriots were heroes in those early days of the Republic. Even I, modest as had been my deeds, was cheered far beyond my deserts, and for Lesba they wove a wreath of flowering laurel, and forced the happy and blushing girl to wear it throughout our progress through the streets of the capital.

Fonseca invited us to the palace, where he had established his headquarters; but we preferred to go to the humbler home of Captain Mazanovitch, wherein we might remain in comparative retirement during the exciting events of those first days of rejoicing.

Afterward we witnessed the grand procession in honor of the Dictator. I remember that Fonseca and his old enemy Piexoto rode together in the same carriage, all feuds being buried in their common triumph. The bluff general wore his most gorgeous uniform and the lean statesman his shabby gray cloak. And in my judgment the adulation of the populace was fairly divided between these two champions, although the Dictator of the Republic bowed with pompous pride to right and left, while the little man who was destined to afterward become President of the United States of Brazil shrank back in his corner with assumed modesty. Yet Piexoto's eyes, shrewd and observing, were everywhere, and it may be guessed that he lost no detail of the day's events.

Paola should have been in that procession, likewise, for the people fairly idolized the former Minister of Police, and both Fonseca and Piexoto had summoned him to join them. But no; he preferred to sit at Valcour's side in a quiet, sunlit room, effacing himself in all eyes but hers, while history was making in the crowded streets of the capital.

It required many days to properly organize a republican form of government; but the people were patient and forbearing, and their leaders loyal and true; so presently order began to come out of chaos.

Meantime Valcour mended daily, and the roses that had so long been strangers to her pale cheeks began to blossom prettily under the influence of Francisco's loving care.

They were happy days, I know; for Lesba and I shared them, although not so quietly. For the dear girl was all aglow with the triumph of Liberty, and dragged me as her escort to every mass-meeting or festival and everyone of the endless processions until the enthusiasm of her compatriots had thoroughly tired me out. The Liberty of Brazil bade fair to deprive me of my own; but I bore the ordeal pretty well, in Lesba's society.

Then came a day when I obtained my reward. Valcour had made a quick recovery, and now needed only the strengthening influence of country air; so one bright morning we all boarded a special train and traveled to Cuyaba, reaching safely the de Pintra mansion in the early evening.

Nothing seemed changed about the dear old place, which I had already arranged to purchase from Dom Miguel's executors. Pedro had resigned his position as station-master to become our major-domo, and the thoughtful fellow had made every provision for our comfort on this occasion of our homecoming.

Captain Mazanovitch was with us. He had retired from active service to enjoy his remaining years in his daughter's society, and although he seldom allowed one of us to catch a glimpse of his eyes, the face of the old detective had acquired an expression of content that was a distinct advantage to it.

I had chosen to occupy my old room off the library, and early on the morning following our arrival I arose and passed out into the shrubbery. Far down the winding walks, set within the very center of the vast flower gardens, was the grave of Dom Miguel, and thither I directed my steps. As I drew near I saw the square block of white marble that the patriots had caused to be erected above the last resting-place of their beloved chieftain. It bore the words

"Miguel De Pintra
Savior of Brazil"

and is to this day the mecca of all good republicans.

Lesba was standing beside the tomb as I approached. Her gown was as white as the marble itself, but a red rose lay upon her bosom and another above Dom Miguel. She did not notice my presence until I touched her arm, but then she turned and smiled into my eyes.

"'Savior of Brazil!'" she whispered softly. "It is splendid and fitting. Did you place it there, Robert?"

"No," I answered; "the credit is due to Piexoto. He claimed the privilege for himself and his associates, and I considered it his right."

"Dear uncle!" said she; and then we turned reverently away and strolled through the gardens. Every flower and shrub lay fair and fresh under the early sun, and we admired them and drank in their fragrance until suddenly, as we turned a corner of the hedge, I stopped and said:

"Lesba, it was here that I first met you; on this exact spot!"

"I remember," said she, brightly. "It was here that I prophesied you would be true to the Cause."

"And it was here that I loved you," I added; "for I cannot remember a moment since that first glimpse of your dear face that my heart has not been your very own."

She grew sober at this speech, and I watched her face anxiously.

"Tell me, Lesba," said I at last, "will you be my wife?"

"And go to your country?" she asked, quickly.

I hesitated.

"All my interests are there, and my people, as well," I answered.

"But I cannot leave Brazil," she rejoined, positively; "and Brazil needs you, too, Robert, in these years when she is beginning to stand alone and take her place among nations. Has not Fonseca offered you a position as Director of Commerce?"

"Yes; I am grateful for the honor. But I have large and important business interests at home."

"But your uncle is fully competent to look after them. You have told me as much. We need you here more than they need you at home, for your commercial connections and special training will be of inestimable advantage in assisting the Republic to build up its commerce and extend its interests in foreign lands. Brazil needs you. *I* need you, Robert! Won't you stay with us—dear? For a time, at least?"

Well, I wrote to Uncle Nelson, and his reply was characteristic.

"I loaned you to de Pintra, not to Brazil," his letter read. "But I am convinced the experiences to be gained in that country, during these experimental years of the new republic, will be most valuable in fitting you for the management of your own business when you are finally called upon to assume it. You may remain absent for five years, but at the expiration of that period I shall retire from active business, and you must return to take my place."

On those terms I compromised with Lesba, and we were married on the same day that Valcour and Francisco Paola became man and wife.

"I should have married you, anyway," Lesba confided to me afterward; "but I could not resist the chance to accomplish one master-stroke for the good of my country." And she knew the compliment would cancel the treachery even before I had kissed her.

As I have hinted, these events happened years ago, and I wonder if I have forgotten any incident that you would be interested to know.

Dom Miguel's old home became our country residence, and we clung to it everyday I could spare from my duties at the capital. It was here our little Valcour was born, and here that Francisco came afterward to bless our love and add to our happiness and content.

The Paolas are our near neighbors, and often Captain Mazanovitch drives over with their son Harcliffe to give the child a romp with our little ones. The old detective is devoted to the whole noisy band, but yesterday I was obliged to reprove Francisco for poking his chubby fingers into the captain's eyes in a futile endeavor to make him raise the ever-drooping lids.

The five-year limit expired long since; but I have never been able to fully separate my interests from those of Brazil, and although our winters are usually passed in New Orleans, where Uncle Nelson remains the vigorous head of our firm, it is in sunny Brazil that my wife and I love best to live.

A Note About the Author

L. Frank Baum (1856–1919) was an American author of children's literature and pioneer of fantasy fiction. He demonstrated an active imagination and a skill for writing from a young age, and was encouraged by his father who bought him the printing press with which he began to publish several journals. Although he had a lifelong passion for theater, Baum found success with his novel *The Wonderful Wizard of Oz* (1900), a self-described "modernized fairy tale" that led to thirteen sequels, inspired several stage and radio adaptations, and eventually, in 1939, was immortalized in the classic film starring Judy Garland.

A Note from the Publisher

Spanning many genres, from non-fiction essays to literature classics to children's books and lyric poetry, Mint Edition books showcase the master works of our time in a modern new package. The text is freshly typeset, is clean and easy to read, and features a new note about the author in each volume. Many books also include exclusive new introductory material. Every book boasts a striking new cover, which makes it as appropriate for collecting as it is for gift giving. Mint Edition books are only printed when a reader orders them, so natural resources are not wasted. We're proud that our books are never manufactured in excess and exist only in the exact quantity they need to be read and enjoyed.

bookfinity™

Discover more of your favorite classics with Bookfinity™.

- Track your reading with custom book lists.
- Get great book recommendations for your personalized Reader Type.
- Add reviews for your favorite books.
- AND MUCH MORE!

Visit **bookfinity.com** and take the fun Reader Type quiz to get started.

Enjoy our classic and modern companion pairings!

9 781513 211787